local gods

by

Mark Hurst

2024

Chapter 1

In his wood-panelled private chambers, located to the rear of Holborn High Court, Judge Archibald Hunter, Archie to his (few) friends, or that 'twisted old fuck' to his (more numerous) enemies, adjusts the starched collar of his shirt and pulls his court robes over his head. The thick red cloth sits heavily on his narrow shoulders as he straightens the neck tabs, so they rest neatly across his upper chest.

He nods approval at his reflection in the mirror, which hangs above his washbasin. His short wig, still the horsehair variety, sits on its stand next to the sink. He allows his hand to touch it fondly but refrains from placing it on his head just yet. These are still the dog days of late summer. The weather is hot and sultry, and his wig has a tendency to upset the heavy psoriasis on his scalp.

He's been looking forward to this day. The third day of the trial, with counsel for the defence up today. He is an old friend from school, a first-rate chap called Rupert Ogilvy. Archie fondly recalls he plays a bloody good straight iron off the tee down at Four Trees, which is itself a splendid place. *Lovely greens and fairways*, he thinks wistfully. *Nice totty behind the bar too, and long may that continue.* Not so long ago, there'd been a petition to allow female admission to the clubhouse, and that would've buggered it up, but Archie and a few of his chums had put paid to that notion. *Some traditions are worth preserving*, he thinks. *In fact, most traditions are worth preserving, although you have to say that quietly these days, lest some callow soul is offended. Besides*, he thinks, it'll be good to see him in action in court. If there's one thing he knows about Rupert, it's he knows how to make them squirm. *The little sluts*, he thinks, with a shiver of delight.

Archibald Hunter is the ripe old age of eighty-three, although he's sure he looks much younger. When he looks in the mirror, he doesn't see pouches of crocodile skin beneath his eyes, nor a flaky scalp that sheds reptilian scales into thin, straggly hair the dirty grey of winter sky. Instead, he sees exactly what he wants to see, as is his way, being a man born of and then steeped in enormous privilege throughout his entire life. He sees youth, he sees vitality. He sees a man who can do whatever he wants. A man answerable to no-one.

He breathes a sigh of contentment, humming tunelessly as he plucks a small gold key from his robe pocket. He unlocks a cabinet that hangs on the wall to one side of his washbasin. Its top shelf is packed full of bottles, each containing a different variety of single malt whisky. He's an avid collector of things, his Nanny used to call him a little squirrel when he was a boy, and it was a habit he's never managed or been inclined to break, even when his tastes grew more expensive, and in some cases, extreme.

He runs a contented hand over the bottles, enjoying the tinkling chorus he creates, but has no desire for their amber contents, at least not now, although he concedes he might treat himself to a nip from one of the special ones later, especially if the day's business goes as well as he hopes. Besides, he thinks, he's more interested in the contents of the other shelf today He breaks into a smile that wouldn't look out of place on a fox loitering outside a henhouse at midnight.

The shelf in question houses several dark brown bottles. Each contains a different type of pill, each serving a different purpose. He thinks the passage of a man's life can be measured by the number of pills required to keep the cogs spinning. They have a habit of creeping into a chap's orbit from around the age of forty, and steadily accumulate thereafter, taking their silent place by the bedside, until the time comes when you practically rattle with the damn things. Happily, even at his age, he's only beholden to a few, principally for blood pressure and cholesterol, which isn't bad, he thinks. An achievement worthy of pride and a differentiator from many of his peers. After all, there aren't many chaps who can still do what he can do by the time they hit their eighties. He puts it down to good genetics. His mother lived until she was well over one hundred, and he fully intends to do the same.

He sweeps up a small brown bottle, rattling it in time with the tune he hums, a percussive accompaniment that brings a smile to his lips, revealing yellowing teeth that lean drunkenly against each other, like a broken picket fence.

He's left his spectacles in his overcoat, so he raises the bottle to his face, squinting so he can read the label, and reminds himself that he'll need to retrieve them before he goes into the courtroom. It's important he selects the right pill. Today of all days.

He is disturbed by a knock on the door to his chambers. 'Fifteen minutes, sir,' says a muffled voice. It is one of the court clerks, calling him to order. His courtroom will be filling up. He doesn't acknowledge the reminder. He likes to keep his crowds waiting anyway. It never hurts to remind the court who is in charge. They will wait. It is his circus.

Archibald thinks Cialis is an enormous improvement on Viagra, offering the same level of rigidity but with far greater control, which is an important upgrade given his social standing. As much as he needs a bit of assistance in that department these days, even when he is lucky enough to sit on what he considers to be a 'juicy' case, it's still a high-risk strategy to welcome an uncontrollable erection into a courtroom. Cialis is different. It allows him to keep his dog on a tight lead, so to speak.

He pours a small glass of water and shakes a single tablet into his palm.

Rupert will do the business he is sure, prying deep, exposing sordid details of the doe-eyed princess for the court. His robes are voluminous enough and his bench suitably sheltered, that prying eyes won't notice how busy his hands become when he listens so intently. Of that, he is sure. Besides, even if anyone did spot a movement that might (incorrectly) be construed as inappropriate, well who would believe it anyway? No-one! Or at least no-one that mattered. This is his court, and within it he is king. He smiles at his reflection in the mirror.

The predilections of Archibald Hunter were well known amongst the legal community. Any defence counsel worth his salt knew that if you were going to take a statutory rape to trial, or any other type of sexual assault for that matter, then you were going to try to list it at Holborn High Court. A defence counsel that teased, prodded, and ultimately humiliated a victim, found favour in the court of Archibald Hunter. Even if a jury's decision went the 'wrong way', well, let's just say his sentencing could be favourable, particularly if a defendant was the 'right sort'.

Archibald tosses the pill into his mouth and knocks it back with a gulp from a glass of water, swallowing it with a grimace. He smooths down his straggly hair, and places his wig carefully onto his head, adjusting it so it's central and firmly seated. Nothing worse than an old judge with a wig like an avalanche, he thinks, makes you look bloody ridiculous.

He claps his hands together, already feeling a familiar stirring at his groin.

It's great to be alive, he thinks!

****

Time's bruising passage has conspired to squeeze Holborn High Court uncomfortably between two 1960s office blocks, forcing its weathered red brickwork, Victorian turrets, and pleasing masonry accoutrements to clash aggressively with ugly grey formed concrete, rendering it like the spine of some ancient leather-bound book that has been misplaced in a library amongst shiny modern texts.

Like many of the crumbling artifices of Britain's Victorian past, it battles to maintain its place amidst a harsh tide of architectural progress and unforgiving planning decisions that have reduced the once uniform streets of London to a tattered hotchpotch of conflicting styles.

The entrance to the court is open. The wheels of justice commence creaking progress, as black-robed barristers hustle through the doorway into a wide lobby. The floor is tiled and footsteps noisy above the hum of conversation. The entrance to the four courtrooms is protected by modern security equipment, not unlike that found at an airport, designed to prevent any further crimes taking place within, should someone decide that the justice offered within these walls was not to their liking. Instances of more primal retribution have happened in the past. Blood has been spilled and shortly afterwards barriers and metal detectors sprouted up from the tiled floor, like alien weed.

Two orderly queues form in that peculiarly British way that requires minimal, if any, obvious instruction. People move into place with a low murmur of assent, like worker bees entering a hive.

The left-hand queue is shorter and moves faster. It's reserved for judicial staff and those lawyers that defend or prosecute the unfortunate souls who are brought in to face justice. The right-hand queue is for the public, the press, and relatives of those who appear before the court. In particularly sensitive cases, and in recognition that emotions can run high, the relatives of defendants and accused are ushered in separately, to avoid any unpleasantness.

The defendants arrive via a private rear entrance, accessed through a side street, where windowless prison vans sweep in, avoiding the flashing cameras of any paparazzi.

There are no paparazzi today. The cases to be heard are on face value unspectacular, just the normal, if unpleasant, consequence of mutual human existence. Nothing of obvious interest. Not to most people anyway.

A man, nondescript, medium height, with dark skin and unremarkable features, joins the right-hand queue in the entrance hall. He's wearing sunglasses. They hide bright green eyes that look out of place in his face, as well they might. They are coloured contact lenses. The queue shuffles forward by inches. Eventually he passes through the security scanner, removing his sunglasses when requested, nodding politely to a faintly harassed security officer, who fails to register the light-fingered removal of his lanyard, but will later recall those vivid green eyes (which was entirely their purpose, to provide a memorable false contrast that eclipses other memory).

Inside Courtroom Number One, the jury files onto benches that bracket the wall on the left-hand side of the room. They shuffle onto the hard seating. The last few days have already been long and littered with distressing evidence. All of them will be happy when it is over.

The famous Rupert Ogilvy KC, he of the first-rate golf swing, sweeps into the courtroom, casts an imperious gaze over the jury, and seats himself at his bench, where he fussily arranges his long black robes around him. Junior barristers scurry this way and that, gathering bundles of paper and placing them reverentially before him.

His defendant, a red-faced young man with a thick neck, a smart tailored suit and tousled blond hair, is led into court by two uniformed police officers and takes his place confidently in the dock. He nods to his family, who are seated towards the rear of the chamber, before returning his steady gaze to the jury. Rupert has counselled him on his demeanour, and suggested he make as much eye contact as he can with the jury, to give them the benefit of his wholesome well-bred gaze. Rupert says he's a fine young fellow, not the type of chap to do anything wrong, not on purpose anyway. This was just horseplay that got out of hand, as it can do when young fellows are having fun. Make the jury see that and you're home and dry, he confidently predicted.

Counsel for prosecution shuffles paperwork on his own table with the air of someone who has lost something but isn't quite sure what. He only has one clerk, and his robes are noticeably less well kept than those of his counterpart. To his left sits a young woman. She is called Lily Proctor.

She's dressed in black, which only serves to heighten the pale, ashen quality of her skin. Her eyes are watery with unshed tears, tears that haven't yet found capacity for exit, as if her pain has fused them within her body. She studies her plain shoes, purposefully avoiding eye contact with the young man in the dock. The young man who violated her, filmed said violation, and then amplified that savage horror by sharing the film online with what felt like the whole universe. She can't bring herself to think his name, never mind say it.

It's her turn to give evidence today. Her counsel squeezes her shoulder, but she finds no comfort in the gesture, she feels as though she's drifting on updraughts of savage fear, that when she is called to the witness stand the floor will vanish beneath her feet and she will fall endlessly. Immediately behind her in the public gallery her parents sit together, leaning into one another, fused by the resin of grim desperation and savage impotence.

The remaining chairs in the courtroom are empty, except for one man who sits at the back, near the door. It is the man with green eyes. He's not known to Lily or her parents, although if they knew what he can do, what he offers, they might have reached out to him for his services, but as good (or bad) fortune would have it depending on your viewpoint, fate has carried him into the courtroom as a friend of a friend, or rather an acquaintance of another who's felt the same savage pain they do. An acquaintance who demands retribution.

'All rise,' booms a voice. The soft murmur within the courtroom dies and Judge Archibald Hunter enters and makes himself comfortable behind his bench. He glances briefly at Rupert, one of his bushy eyebrows dancing up his forehead.

'The defence calls Lily Proctor...' says Rupert. His face is cast in a stern but sympathetic, almost parental, frown as he watches Lily rise from her seat and walk on mermaids' feet to the dock. She pauses only briefly to transmit a frozen glance to her parents, who nod white-knuckled support.

Archibald settles back in his chair.

Rupert Ogilvy stands behind his desk, looking down at paperwork he moves thoughtfully across its polished surface. The expectant silence of the courtroom is a springboard for his words. Without looking up he says, 'Do you consider yourself a woman to whom moral standards are important, Lily...?

Archibald supresses a smile. A hand steals beneath his gown and his heartbeat quickens as he settles in for the show.

****

Archibald makes himself comfortable in his old leather club chair. It's positioned near the fireplace in his chambers. One of his clerks has set the fire, and it pops and fizzes most agreeably. He's removed his robe and wig and sits in an untucked white shirt and dark trousers, the inside of which are still sticky with his cooling seed. A cut crystal glass

10

containing amber liquid sits in one hand. His other hand restlessly caresses the old leather.

What a show that was, he thinks with a contented sigh. *The videos of the little minx, good God. Who would have thought such a demure little thing was capable of such things!* He speculates it's possible he didn't even need Cialis today. And those tears, the racking sobs that accompanied the grunting and groaning images, the shame she radiated, as Rupert so expertly shared her social media history, her OnlyFans account, short-lived though it was, the prosecution protested – only a few weeks to help fund her studies! Or so she said, the delicious little slut! *Simply marvellous stuff.*

Archie decides he owes Rupert a special thank you, especially as he thinks the jury were a little unconvinced. There were a few too many women amongst their number to be sure of a not guilty verdict and he wasn't confident that Rupert's shots, as well crafted as they were, had all hit the target. No matter, he thinks, even if the young fella finds himself out of favour with the jury, well it's his first offence, no reason to punish such a fine fellow from a good family, when his reputation was already tarnished by such a dreadful experience.

Archibald contents himself that the justice he decides to dispense will be appropriate. He rubs a hand across his face. *The young chap was a good looker too,* he thinks, solid rugby type that he'd favoured himself when he was at school. He wasn't beyond a fumble with a beautiful boy if the chance arose. *I'm an equal opportunity deviant!* he thinks with a throaty chuckle.

He tosses back whisky with a small gasp of pleasure and pours himself another nip, before nestling back into his chair. A rattle on the door to his chambers stirs him from his thoughts.

'My Lord,' says a soft voice. 'My Lord, I'm sorry to disturb you in your chambers at this late hour...'

Archibald scoots around in his seat, the old leather squeaking in protest. A young man dressed in black barristers' robes is standing in his doorway. He doesn't recognise him, but it isn't unusual for the pupils to come visit him, asking for advice on a legal matter and so on, and he is always happy to help, sometimes for a price. He thinks a bit of quid pro quo wouldn't go amiss today. Lily Proctor has gotten him quite worked up, and his own hand, as skilled as it is, well it doesn't always cut it, does it!? He drags a lizard tongue over dry lips.

'My dear fellow,' he says. 'Please come in, no problem at all! And it's not Lord! My goodness, no, I am but a humble High Court judge, the title of Lord eludes me still,' he says with faux modesty. 'I was just sitting here savouring a drop of God's finest liquid and ruminating on the day's events. One of Rupert's pupils, are you? Pull up a chair if you wish,' he says, gesturing to the one opposite him, 'I have nowhere special to be this evening...'

The man sits himself down and smiles. Archibald notices he has the most striking bright green eyes. 'Would you care for a drop? It's single malt, from a little distillery I know up in Dornoch. Very exclusive. My wife always tells me it's better not to drink alone...'

'Why not. That'd be nice. Thanks.'

Archie totters over to his shelves, running a theatrical hand over the rows of old books, and finds another glass into which he pours a healthy slug of whisky. He hands it to his visitor, allowing his fingers to stray lightly across his hand when he takes it from him. Archie makes eye contact with him and feels a delicious spike of excitement.

'So, what shall I call you then? You've not introduced yourself...' says Archie.

'No, I haven't, have I?' says the young man. 'Sometimes anonymity is better, don't you think?'

'Well, quite,' says Archie, his voice not quite steady. *This is a feisty one* he thinks, *straight to the point, and all the better for it. Secrets!* He has a few of them, as this young buck will swiftly discover! The Cialis is kicking in again. His old snake is uncurling fast, throbbing in time with a rapidly increasing heartbeat and Archie wonders, not for the first time, if he should be a little more careful about the amount of pressure he is putting through his old pump. A quick glance at those fascinating green eyes allows him to dismiss the thought. That concern is for another day.

'Your reputation around the court is, let's say, interesting,' says the man.

'Interesting?' replies Archie. 'Is that all! If that is a word you might ascribe to me, it feels a rather damming assessment. As you get old you prefer more colourful description, but for now at least it allows me to pose a question. Are you *interested*, my young friend?' Archie can't tell how old this one is, but they are all young to him. He has a face that's curiously difficult to pin down, almost as if he is a blur, a phantom, other than those bright green eyes of course. There is no forgetting those.

'I wouldn't be here if I wasn't,' he replies and Archie decides this dance has gone on long enough. One of the few advantages of age is the permission it grants for impatience, he thinks. There's no time to waste, get what you want while you still have the wit and will to do so, that's his motto!

He levers himself up from his chair. His trousers totem-pole in front of him and he fumbles at his waist, releasing the catch and pulling down his zipper. The trousers fall softly to his ankles, revealing a throbbing erection, bouncing up proudly from a forest of white hair. He never wears underwear, restrictive and unhelpful as it is when he wants easy access to himself in the courtroom.

His breath whistles between his teeth like an old kettle. 'Hurry up then, boy,' he says.

The young man rises from his chair and takes a slow step towards him. The light of the fire flickers in his eyes. Archie's balls, which hang somewhere between his knees, cry out for attention, and he mutters a breathless plea for service.

'I understand you're a nasty old man...are you?' he says. A hand grabs Archie's erect penis firmly, very firmly in fact. Firm enough to hurt. He draws in a sharp breath.

'Gently...' gasps Archie.

The young man brings his other hand around and Archie groans even louder, enjoying the pain, working himself up to an inevitable release. He can feel familiar tension in his thighs and his eyes roll back in his head.

His gurgling pleasure is replaced by an ice-cold sheet of pain, swiftly followed by a rush of heat, exploding at his groin, but witnessed down the front of his legs.

'What the...' he wheezes.

The man steps back. One hand holds a razor blade. In the other is approximately three inches of Archibald Hunter's severed penis.

Archie's mouth drops open as if on a hinge, but no sound comes out. His heart roars in his chest. At his groin, blood fountains from his sliced appendage, a fire hose of liquid pumping thickly out of artificially swollen arteries that force fed his penis. It splatters down his skinny legs, turning the floor slick. His knees tremble, as if troubled by a strong wind, and he slowly drops to his knees.

'The pills you take; they bring unforeseen consequence. Your heart beats very strongly doesn't it, quite hard to slow it down, I'd imagine? I can hear it from here.'

Archie clutches a hand to his chest, where a racehorse heart hammers away, each thud coinciding with a fountain of blood from his severed appendage. 'Why...' he gasps.

'Someone wants you to pay for what you've done. To mothers, to sisters, to daughters. I'm here to deliver the invoice, so to speak.'

The man smiles. He places a finger delicately into Archie's open mouth and pushes the dead end of the severed penis between his gaping jaws. Archie gags weakly and slumps backwards against his chair, his knees sliding out in front of him in the slick pool of blood, like an ancient footballer celebrating a goal.

The man takes a seat in one of the leather chairs and watches him die. He then takes a picture with a disposable camera. The flash pops. He takes another one, moving a bit closer so as to get a better angle of Archie's almost comically surprised face. The camera is returned to his pocket. It will be posted to his nanny for onward transmission to the client once payment is confirmed.

He removes the barristers' robes that he procured from a cupboard in a locker room on the ground floor. He stuffs them inside a small holdall he left by the door. They will be burned later, along with everything else associated with this job.

He takes a moment to remove the crystal glass he'd been given. He places it into a clear zip bag and tucks it into the side pocket of his holdall. The scalpel smeared with blood joins it. Finally, he wipes clean the arms of the chair he sat in, running a cloth over the leather, paying particular attention to the ends where there is a small risk of prints, notwithstanding the gloves he wears. You can't be too careful in this business.

He didn't touch anything else during his short time in the room but gives all the other surfaces a careful wipe anyway, until he is content no further remediation is required. He knows there are no CCTV cameras in Archie's chambers, which is not a surprise given what the nasty old bastard liked to get up to in here, he thinks, but there are cameras in other parts of the building, so he needs to be careful.

He glances at Archie's corpse and grimaces. The coup de grâce was not planned. The Cialis combined with additional medication he has in his pocket, which he'd planned to slip into his whisky, was meant to have triggered a massive and fatal heart attack, but in the moment it hadn't felt enough. He wanted him to suffer, to know he'd been caught. He wonders if he might regret this lapse of judgement. *No matter*, he thinks. *What's done is done.*

It's time to go.

Chapter 2

We'll call him Pete.

It's a name he's using for now and as far as he's concerned it's as good as any other. He's not a sentimental man, which is probably just as well, given his chosen vocation.

His handler, who calls himself Dave but is almost certainly not called Dave, sits opposite him at a table in a quiet pub, constructed sometime around 1960 in a fading sink estate just outside Bromley By Bow. The table is old and battle scarred, covered in numerous circular rings burned into the veneer by pint glasses over the course of half a century. The curtains are faded and smell of tobacco smoke and cooking fat, despite the fact the smoking ban means no-one has smoked a cigarette in the pub for over twenty years. The windows are opaque, offering a ghostly view of a shattered high street that could be anywhere.

Whilst the décor could do with an upgrade, these characteristics are the reason Dave arranges to meet him there. It's nowhere, there's no CCTV either inside or outside in the streets that surround it. It's a part of London that no-one important cares about, which means it's as invisible as the people that make it home, an increasingly rarity in a part of a world that's become a playground for the rich. Even if anyone did see them, the patrons of this establishment in Tower Hamlets are on the right side of the line. They don't speak to anyone. Ever.

Pete doesn't know Dave's real name, and he's not interested in knowing it, or anything else about him, never once in the ten years they've been associated. It's just part of the protocol. Simple and effective for as many years as anyone with an ounce of common sense can remember. The less you know, the less chance you (or anyone else) are going to get caught. Dave is just a link in a long chain, a dead drop, the mechanism that is industry standard in professional circles.

Only amateurs or idiots conducted business otherwise, and Pete's no idiot. That behaviour was left to so-called 'hard men', the type who'd offer to sort someone out for you after a few beers in the pub. The type of fellas who always proclaimed to know someone who could fix things. Maybe they did, maybe they didn't, but if you wanted something done, or rather someone done, you were well advised to keep clear of the 'hard men' of this world. Hard men just meant hard time, as the saying went.

Pete doesn't know how clients are routed through the complicated machinery of the underworld, through various dead drops until their instructions get to Dave, his handler, or Nanny as they are commonly known, as in Mary Poppins.

He just knows having a good Nanny is as essential to a productive professional life as breathing. A good one, one you can trust (insofar as you trusted anyone in the life) is everything. Pete trusts 'Dave', as much as he needs to, and that's all that matters. He's the last cog in a wheel, the only piece of machinery Pete has to interact with and understand. Dave provides instruction, Dave arranges payment, Dave keeps his mouth shut. It's worked like clockwork, the difference between famine and feast, and the last ten years without any trouble is testament to that.

Dave takes a sip from a pint glass that looks as if it might've seen the inside of a dishwasher in about 2010. He grimaces at the bitter taste of suspiciously flat, lifeless lager. It looks like the type of drink that's already pre-booked you a distressing night on the toilet. He primly pushes it away from himself, and the half-drunk glass sits between them like an accusation.

'There's been a fair amount of heat,' says Dave. He waits for a reply that doesn't come. He sighs. 'I suppose that was always a risk. They don't like it when it's one of their own. From what I've heard the dirty old bastard got what was coming to him.'

'Guess so,' says Pete.

'You guess so?' says Dave with a raised eyebrow. 'I don't recall anything in your instructions about choking the fucker on his own cock? Seems like you've exercised a degree of artistic licence, and it's stirred things up. The great and the good aren't going to let it drop, not for a while. You need to get out of town, at least for a while anyway...'

It's always 'They' isn't it, Pete thinks. The perpetual war between the haves and the have nots that's entwined within the DNA of the British. The old class system was alive and in rude health. Social mobility was as much a myth as the American dream, and was sold just as rigorously, albeit with less overt fanfare. The bitter squeeze that followed the pandemic has only served to make it worse. The country is a fucking mess, but Dave is right, 'they' would find the resources to hunt down the killer of a good ole boy like Archibald Hunter. He was establishment, and establishment demanded retribution.

Pete pushes his own pint glass around the table, dragging a snail trail of liquid across the burnished surface. The pale froth of his bitter looks as unappetising as Dave's flat lager. A feeling of disquiet settles over him. The flourish he added to this job was a mistake. He's still not sure what came over him. It was meant to be a poisoning, a heart attack. He knew about Archie's predilections, knew that the pills he took would make the dose lethal, but something had come over him. Cutting off his cock just seemed like the right thing to do in the moment. He now regrets the lapse of judgement. It was unprofessional, and Dave's comment, although laced with a mock joviality, serves as a clear rebuke for his mistake. He should've known better.

'Understood,' says Pete.

'You still Dawn?' asks Dave. Levity is gone. His face is a cold mask, all business.

'Yeah, still Dawn,' replies Pete.

'Dawn' they say. A person was dawn if they were reliable. As reliable as day following night, as reliable as the dawn. If you're not reliable you might find yourself not anything. A chain is only as strong as each of its links, and a weak link is replaced, disposed of without mercy. Pete knows contractors disappear if things go wrong. As clichéd as it was, the streets did indeed have a voice, and it was clear. You fuck up once, not even once too often, just once, then you'll find yourself disappeared. The Nannies know how to make the medicine go down; it's part of their job.

'I know a place you can hole up. Out of the way. Quiet. I'll send you details. Do yourself a favour and get yourself lost. I'll contact you if anything comes up,' says Dave.

'I guess I could do with a break,' says Pete.

'You guess right. I'll have my ear to the ground on this one. But I want you out.'

'Fine,' says Pete.

Dave nods. He takes one further sip from his pint, grimaces and pushes back his chair. 'Fucking beer in this place tastes like shit,' he says. He puts his coat on. From a pocket he fishes out a mobile phone, still in its box. He puts it on the table in front of Pete. 'For when we need to get in touch,' he says. 'Until next time...'

Pete nods. They don't shake hands. Dave leaves without looking back. The barman wanders over.

'That dead?' he says, pointing at Dave's half-empty pint glass, and Pete nods. The man sweeps it up in a meaty hand and returns to his place behind an empty bar. The pint is given a cursory wash under a tap that howls like a whipped dog, before being placed back on a high shelf. Pete can still see greasy fingerprints tattooed on its side.

He sits back in his chair, stretches out his legs and releases a sigh that fails to dispel his unease. He's not in a rush, despite Dave's instruction. It's time to reflect, he thinks. It's good discipline, after any job, good or bad. And this one's feeling a lot like bad. He shakes his head, as if to clear sticky thoughts.

There's no-one he can talk to. No friends, and no family, not anymore. He's yet to locate a self-help forum for contract killers.

His real parents are long dead, passing within six months of each other when he was still a boy. He'd buried his mother alone and hadn't even attended his father's funeral. He'd been an unpleasant man, a father in name only, a red-faced, bitter drunk. His mother had the misfortune to meet him when he was posted overseas. She'd been cajoled back to East London, saying farewell to distant shores and warm breezes, exchanging them for cold concrete and grey sky, with the promise of a good life with a good man. He then began a slow reverse metamorphosis, from butterfly back to cocoon, becoming a dry, angry husk. The only sorrow in his death was that it came too late. The six months it allowed his saintly mother to live without his brooding presence was nowhere near enough to repay the misery he'd inflicted upon her.

As a minor, alone and adrift, he was catapulted into the care system, a brand-new circle of hell, one where the man he'd become was ultimately forged. Those three years had been unpleasant, but his memory of foster brothers and sisters has all the emotional resonance of passengers with whom he shared a bus, one that trundled towards an inevitable, time-limited destination, ejecting one or another at various places en route, when the state's slim obligation was fulfilled. Those faces, those moments, were forever lost in the rear-view mirror of his life, and that suited him well.

Popular culture would have it that your average contract killer was either some form of human debris, washed along by a mysterious tide that runs outside the tick tock of normal life, or a jacked-up superhuman, capable of taking down an army of bad guys in a heartbeat. He's yet to meet the latter outside of a cinema screen, and it irks him mightily that his own life seems to fit the former stereotype quite neatly.

Fate inflicts wounds on all of us, he thinks, you just have to hope they heal, and the scars are well hidden.

He counts himself lucky. His misfortune hasn't led him to be flushed into any of the various institutional toilets society reserves for those who fall between the cracks. He's avoided jail, he avoided military service, thus discounting another cliché that would've had him taught how to point a gun and squeeze a trigger under the direction of some red-faced lunatic screaming orders for queen and country.

Pete just discovered he could kill things. People, to be precise.

Dave says it's a gift, and although he's not sure he would describe it as such, he begrudgingly admits it's allowed him to find a niche in life that suits his characteristics, and isn't that what most folks are looking for? He has a memory of filling out one of those career questionnaires at his high school, on a rare occasion he'd attended, the ones where you coloured in little sausage shapes in response to multiple choice questions, with the promise that your destiny would be revealed. The list of suitable jobs it spat out, a roll call for the mundane and mindless, had been as meaningless as the lessons he studiously avoided, but one characteristic it identified from his scribbled choices stayed with him. It said he was patient and so well suited to monotonous repetitive tasks. His jaded teacher (and they were all jaded, vaguely sepia-toned nobodies in his memory) proclaimed a life on a factory production line awaited him. Someone laughed, but he didn't care. It turns out killing folks was often monotonous work, and required infinite patience, at least if you didn't want to get caught.

Pete looks around the bar. A new customer has arrived, a weary looking man in a high-vis jacket emblazoned with his employer's name. He slumps onto a stool. A pint is placed in front of him without prompting. He wears a face mask, which he pulls below his chin. He swallows about half, returns the mask and stares into space.

Dave hasn't said where he's going to send him, but Pete hopes it's away. He feels a need to leave the rot of London. It's always been home, but whatever shine briefly burnished the city back in 2012, when the Olympics made the old whore look like an inclusive, exciting metropolis, has long since passed.

Its streets are choked. Its cold veneer of exclusion re-established, reinforced, like concrete's been poured around its heart, a concrete only permeable by the rich, who still breeze around within their bubble of affluence, not seeing the discord around them, the crumbling infrastructure they don't use, the beaten-up public services they never access. The country is a fucking shambles, visible to all, unless you've always been rich enough to not notice the difference.

Pete knows what poor feels like. The experience taught him poverty has no nobility. The outdated idea that destitution creates a cradle of the worthy poor, good-hearted folk who look after each other, like community exists and its dim spark provides enough heat to warm hearts, to fill hungry bellies. It isn't true. Human nature is survival. Sometimes that requires collaboration, sometimes it doesn't, but collaboration isn't the same thing as community.

The estate he'd grown up in had been a jungle, a place to refine those survival skills, to make acquaintances that served purpose, but no more than that. If a better time had ever existed, one where people checked on their neighbours, knew everyone's name and all that nonsense, that had long since passed. It was a politician's wet dream, a convenient excuse for leaving those in need well alone. He thinks about the faded rainbows that were born out of Covid, where rich people clapped, and proclaimed we were all in it together, even as they filled their pockets.

He's earned a great deal of money from fulfilling his various contracts. Most of it never touches the UK, funnelling instead through various jurisdictions until it lands in a corporate account managed in Cayman, by some faceless bureaucrat that didn't even pretend to ask questions about its provenance. He's experienced an occasional twinge of guilt, like a nagging toothache provoked by a curious tongue, but he'd grown hard. There were zero saints in this world, just different degrees of devil.

He sighs again. It's a day for them, it seems.

Pete knows he'll go wherever Dave sends him. What else can he do? he muses. He's trapped in a box of his own making.

Chapter 3.

Leaving home is a process that requires more than the simple passing of miles. Distance on its own does not serve to remove the weight of the everyday from a traveller's shoulders. That burden is a complex one, a geological accumulation of many things, each with a different level of viscosity, adhesion and depth. The things that made you, cling to you like bindweed, holding you back, pushing you forward, but never really letting you go.

Pete sits in a window seat on a train, in standard class. It's due to depart from London Paddington to its destination Moreton-in-Marsh at 14.47, but predictably it doesn't.

He's decided to travel light. He carries only a small rucksack, stuffed with a few changes of clothing and his laptop, but he feels heavy. The weight of Dave's admonishment, or more accurately his failure, hangs on his shoulders, so even after he's tucked the bag into the overhead bin, it feels as though he still has it on. The rucksack straps hang down over his seat like drab confetti, but he can't be bothered to tuck them in.

He shares his table with two other passengers. An older lady sits opposite him, her head already buried in a book. He can feel her bony knee pressing against his own beneath the table. Sitting next to her is a young woman, her face predictably captivated by a mobile phone. He's been through the pantomime of exchanging conciliatory smiles and small talk. The relief that neither showed any interest in progressing that interaction is still with him. The seat next to him is currently unoccupied, although the digital display says it's reserved from Oxford.

At least I can spread out a little for now, he thinks. The seats on this train could charitably be described as 'snug'. A scandal considering the price.

He opens his laptop as a voice crackles over a tannoy.

'Ladies and gentlemen, on behalf of Great Western Railway, we would like to apologise for the ongoing delay, this is a result of signal issues just outside of London Paddington. We hope to be underway shortly, and we apologise for any inconvenience the disruption to your journey today will cause you...'

The voice doesn't sound sorry. It just sounds bored, resigned even. He hears a few groans in the carriage and a vague attempt at gallows humour from one passenger who mutters something about leaves on the line. The murmur of discontent subsides, and Pete stares out the window, lost in thought. The platform is an ebbing tide of people, scattered with fluttered farewells, smiles and frowns, occasional tears. It thins slowly, to the tune of the piercing whistle of a platform guard.

He observes a thickset man in a pinstriped suit, a bottle of red wine in hand, arguing with a harassed train guard. The man barks something unpleasant, spittle flying from thick lips as he pushes past him and heads down the platform. He catches Pete's gaze and flares his eyes dramatically in the manner of '*What you looking at?!?* Pete takes in his flushed face and unsteady gait. He sighs and taps at the keyboard on his laptop. The screen springs to life. He pretends to read an article on a website but finds his eyes wander over words without recognition, like a stranger at a dinner party, politely trying to ingratiate himself. Time passes.

'Ladies and gentlemen, I am pleased to announce we now have clearance and will be underway shortly. We are just awaiting our signal and should be on the move in the next five minutes or so. Thank you for your patience and we hope you are enjoying your journey with Great Western Railway this morning...'

A half-hearted cheer rolls around the carriage. Pete catches the eye of the lady opposite, who looks up briefly from her book. They exchange a polite smile of solidarity, and he feels a (very) faint swell of something good, maybe even optimism. He snares it and tries to remind himself that maybe it's not all bad after all. That not everyone on this rock is an arsehole, that some folks are worth saving, despite often-overwhelming evidence to the contrary.

The train jerks forward, starting its stately progress out of the darkness of the station. It gathers speed, no longer click-clacking leisurely as it moves over points, instead settling into a juddering hum as it reaches cruising speed. The concrete monoliths of central London give way to ordered rows of terraced housing, the spaces between them expanding until eventually green fields appear, and the sky starts to breathe again.

A green and pleasant land rolls past his window as if an old picture reel, flashing an idyllic past of chequered fields, undulating crops. Green places where the type of people he grew up with don't get the chance to tread. The warm glow of optimism fades from Pete's consciousness as quickly as it arrived. He runs a hand over his face to smooth away the exhaustion he associates with his rollercoaster outlook. He knows he's the worst kind of people's champion. Stuffed with rage at the injustice of it all, but singularly doing nothing about it.

The train races on and Pete submerges himself in its hypnotic progress. He thinks about what makes him who he is, what allows him to do what he does. He forms a mental check list of ingredients that, when combined, become a recipe for a killer.

Patience is key. In the idle hours he can maintain patience, an eye for detail that isn't softened by the slow tick of time, by fatigue or self-doubt. His father would've called it discipline, he was big on that, and maybe it was, but either way it spoke of control, of yourself, of the minutia that might influence outcomes. Impatience, he's learned, is the cousin of sloppiness, and sloppiness is death.

Then there's paranoia. The unwanted gift you get for surviving the care system. You trust no-one. You have faith in nothing, you assume nothing. You rely only on yourself and your instincts. Embrace that, absorb it into your being and move forward. If it makes for a solitary, lonely existence, embrace that too or give up, there is no viable compromise.

He is good at being invisible. Not that he's a master of disguise (à la Tom Cruise in Ethan Hawke mode) or has some deep specialist knowledge of camouflage, it just turns out he's exceptional at being unexceptional. There's nothing memorable about him. If there'd been a category in his school yearbook for least likely to be remembered, a photo of his gap-toothed grin and fuzzy black hair would have sat proudly above it. Being unmemorable is now a useful thing.

Finally, there's the bit he'd got wrong on Archie Hunter. You don't have an opinion. You don't have a line you won't cross or a cause. You don't take sides; you don't second-guess instructions. You don't have a moral code. You toss that stuff in the bin, close the lid, and bury it deep. You ignore muffled voices that pipe up in the hours before dawn. Empathy is weakness. The minute you care, you're vulnerable. Either do the job or don't do it, but once you've committed, see it through, whoever or whatever the target is.

Pete has killed men and women. Possibly children, but if so, only by accident or association. He's not proud of that, but neither does he allow himself to feel guilt. It's a job.

Once you've got all these basic ingredients packed into a shape you could now only charitably describe as human, you're then concerned with the mechanics of death. The how, not the why.

These are the practical things. Some of them learned, some innate.

Perhaps the hardest thing, he thinks, at least the first few times, is living with the consequence of what you've done. When you look a person in the eyes, another human, witness their final thoughts ricocheting around in real time, eyes darting left and right, when you've heard every cry for clemency. That is a different ball game. Being content that your next minor physical action will end all that person is, ever was and ever will be. It becomes impossibly difficult for some, physical movement stymied by psychological restraints hardwired into DNA, like an invisible moral straitjacket. It becomes a big deal, the biggest of deals, the deadliest of sins. Or at least it did for most people. But it never did for Pete. He just did it and moved on.

Death itself could be delivered in a myriad of ways. A true expert is comfortable with them all. A handgun, a rifle, these rudimentary tools all need to be mastered, but an expert thinks beyond what can be slotted into his hand. There was false comfort in sophisticated weaponry. It didn't make an idiot smart, nor did it make a weak man strong. The opposite was more likely true.

Then there are the more 'creative' techniques. Poisonings, drownings, fatal accidents, cut brakes, explosive cookers. Pete thinks almost anything can be an instrument of death if a little imagination is applied. He finds the absurdity of it strangely pleasing.

Pete's done it all during his 'career' but as his days around the sun increase in number, he is thinking that distance is now his best friend on a job. The further away from a target, the further you are away from the kill and all the consequences that flow from it. Like most true professionals he prefers the quiet solitude of a well-prepared shot from range. Up close and personal is different. Hard, unpredictable, and dangerous. You have to teach yourself to become comfortable with that proximity, where you get to see the lights go out, where your ability to dissociate is tested, but he'd take a cold room, with a clear shot, over a knife fight any day of the week.

A commotion drags him back to the surface. The red-faced man he'd spotted on the platform back in London barges into the carriage. He gives the automatic door an angry kick when it bounces back on his sizeable rump. In one hand he still holds a bottle of red wine. He steadies himself and peers down the carriage, a hunter in pursuit of his quarry. Pete's heart sinks as he observes him spot the empty seat next to him and make unsteady progress towards him.

The man gives the reservation sign above the empty seat a cursory glance, followed by a chuckle that says all that needs to be said, before dropping himself heavily into the seat next to Pete. He's a big guy, and he fills the seat, thick thighs pushing into Pete's legs, squeezing him unapologetically against the window. The bottle of wine is slammed onto the table. He smells like yesterday's office party. He unscrews the bottle and takes a swig. The ladies opposite sink into their seats, holding up phone and book respectively, like shields.

'You alright, mate,' he says loudly, pushing an elbow into Pete's side for emphasis.

'I said y'alright...' followed by a muttered, 'you fuckin twat.'

He turns his attention to the young girl opposite him. 'Hello, darlin',' he says. 'Want a drink?' He waves the wine bottle in her direction. The girl directs her gaze down at the phone in her hand. 'Fucks sake, what's the matter with you lot...' he spits. The girl flashes a desperate glance at Pete, which he absorbs with a blank face.

The man continues to swig from his wine bottle and Pete wonders if he'll pass out at some point. For now he is busily looking around the carriage, his eyes seeking mischief, so respite seems some time away.

A meaty elbow reacquaints itself with Pete's side. The elbow digs in again, and then again. Pete chews the inside of his mouth. His journey out of London is to get away from trouble, not find more of it. He takes a deep breath. On its fourth visit Pete decides he's had enough, and it's necessary to make an intervention. He catches the elbow on its ascent. It ratchets to a halt, strains briefly, before Pete lets it go.

The man offers him a blank stare that is presumably designed to intimidate. His lips flicker back from his teeth, exposing a flash of wine-stained veneers. 'Fucking problem, mate?' he snarls.

'Not yet,' says Pete mildly.

The man narrows his eyes, starting a bleary wine-stained risk assessment. He doesn't realise quite how important that assessment is to his chances of making it off the train in one piece, but then it's not every day you decide to pick a fight with a killer.

Pete isn't, in truth, much to look at, not at first glance anyway, and certainly not to an amateur like this idiot. He isn't built, thick-necked or even obviously muscular. He is lean, but in a wiry way that makes him look like one of those marathon runners. This fool won't be the first to underestimate him, and although professionally that was kind of the idea, in circumstances like this it can be unhelpful. He'd prefer this man got the message and backed off. His natural camouflage is making that outcome less likely, and that isn't ideal.

The seconds spin out. Pete observes uncertainty flickering around the edges of the man's hardened expression, betrayed by a slight tremble along his jaw line. He's wondering (correctly) if he's picked the wrong skinny bloke to try to pick a fight with. He's wondering if this is the kind of sport he's really looking for on a Saturday afternoon.

Common sense prevails, and he offers a derisive snort and makes a display of taking a big swig from the wine bottle, which is now half empty.

Some forty minutes pass, and his table feels like an intake of breath. Everyone is busily avoiding eye contact. By now the man has progressed past mild drunkenness to something else. His eyes are heavy, hooded and offer a piggy mean-spiritedness. He attempts conversation across the aisle with another passenger, but the man puts his headphones in and studiously ignores him. He mutters to himself.

The train starts to slow. The countryside outside the window gives way to an industrial estate and then housing. The tannoy announces they will shortly be arriving at Oxford.

The man finishes his wine, flipping back his head to tease out the last few drops. He looks unhappy and pushes the empty bottle between his hands for a moment before launching himself up from his seat. He wanders off down the train carriage, and Pete can feel a collective sigh of relief from those passengers around him.

When the train stops there is a brief flurry of activity. People getting on and off, bags being hefted into overhead bins, the usual apologetic polite fanfare of 'I think you might possibly be sitting in my seat...' An elderly gentleman works his way down the carriage, peering at the seat numbers, clutching a ticket in his hand. When he reaches Pete, he checks his ticket and breathes a sigh of relief. He smiles politely at them and settles down, making himself comfortable. Pete thinks he looks like a tortoise in his plaid jacket and dark brown corduroy trousers. Pete also thinks he might yet have cause not to get too comfy in his seat if the drunken man returns. He can see the same thought occurring to the ladies sitting opposite. The old man plucks a phone from his pocket and pops a pair of spectacles on, perching them on the end of his nose.

The train eases out of the station. Out of the window, houses swap places with trees again, there are flashes of red and gold amongst the foliage in the low mellow sunshine, a reminder that autumn is in the post. The serenity they offer is short-lived. Pete spies the man bouncing back up the train carriage. He's found the buffet car and unsurprisingly has refreshed his bottle of wine. As he gets closer, he spots the change in circumstances. His eyes narrow and his face reddens. This, thinks Pete, is going to get messy.

'Oi – you, yes fucking you! What you doing in my seat?' he shouts. The old man doesn't even look up, blissfully unaware he's found himself in the crosshairs. He arrives at the table and slams the bottle down, making the young girl jump. The old man looks up, his mouth a perfect O of surprise.

'I said, what... are....you...doing....in my fucking seat.' He emphasises each word with a jabbing finger. Passengers in the rest of the carriage turn to watch events unfurl, with a level of discretion directly correlated to proximity and so the risk of getting involved. Those further away are less cautious. Pete sees a few people filming on their phones, the implication of which make his own choices more difficult.

'I...I, I'm not sure I know what you're talking about, I got on at Oxford, and this is my reservation,' stammers the old man. He reaches into his pocket and pulls out his ticket. 'Here, you see, I have a ticket,' he says.

'I don't give a shit about your ticket. I was sat here, and you've nicked my spot. Now get up before I fucking make you...'

The old man casts a helpless glance around the table. 'There might be some other seats, further down,' he offers, looking hopefully down the carriage for the presence of authority, maybe a train guard, or anyone who will assume responsibility.

'I don't want any other seat, I want my seat,' says the drunk man. Pete can see he's enjoying this sport, finding the victim much more to his liking. He glances at Pete as if testing his resolve to intervene. At this point, and particularly given the number of spectators, he offers nothing but a blank gaze. The young girl opposite chances a comment.

'He has a ticket, it's his seat. Go and find somewhere else and stop bothering him, won't you,' she says, her voice tight and high in her throat. The old lady next to her nods her assent, offering support and then staring at Pete in an attempt to get him to reciprocate.

'You can fuck off as well,' says the man. He spins around and yells at the spectators in the rest of the carriage. 'You can all fuck off!' Heads dip down and eyes are averted. Pete thinks there are few things more likely to bring out the great British reserve than an altercation that risks involving you.

The drunk grabs the old man by the sleeve of his jacket, lifting him roughly to his feet. The girl opposite cries out in alarm, setting off a chorus of disapproval from the watching passengers.

Pete stands. 'Here,' he says. 'Take my seat.'

The girl and the old lady look at him with open-mouthed incredulity. The drunk man smirks. 'Tell you what,' he sneers, 'The oldie can just shift up, and I'll have my old seat back. All the better to enjoy the company of the young lady.' He snorts laughter, eyeing Pete with contempt, and a vague tinge of disappointment that he hadn't realised earlier that the skinny bloke was a walkover after all.

Pete moves out of his seat, past the old man, who meekly and with a wide-eyed look settles into the space he vacated. The drunk man makes sure his shoulder knocks into him as he walks past. The girl can barely bring herself to look at him and Pete is annoyed to feel a flush of shame. 'Thanks a lot,' she hisses.

He knows it's the right decision, but it burns. He can feel the righteous judgment of the other passengers observing events, a righteousness that does not, of course, extend to getting involved themselves, happy as they are to place that burden firmly on his shoulders.

Pete reaches across the table and grabs his rucksack from the overhead bin. He places one arm through the straps, hefts it onto his shoulder and walks away, pushing a button that makes the sliding door between the carriages judder open. He hears pealing laughter as the door closes behind him. It makes him wince, but he knows he made the right call. The professional call.

He stops in the vestibule between carriages and takes a shuddering breath.

To his left is the toilet, one of those ones with the big sliding doors, that remind him of those old sci-fi shows. He puts his rucksack on the floor and sits on it, shuffling a bit to get comfortable. At rush hour this narrow corridor would be crammed with commuters, but at this time of day, and post pandemic it is deserted. Pete is grateful for the solitude. As illustrated by the last hour or so, being around people is exhausting. He is more certain than ever that his trip to the Cotswolds, or more accurately to a place in the absolute arse end of nowhere, is what he needs to refresh and recharge. His head feels overstuffed, his thoughts spilling out, dragging with them the tendrils of other, darker stuff, stuff he works hard to keep buried.

He grimaces, acid burning up his throat, and rummages in a side pocket of the rucksack for his meds. He's been taking Omeprazole for years, his gut is a barren wasteland, scorched earth where nothing natural grew. He pictures a fizzing pool of brackish fluid, popping and bubbling away. He dry-swallows the tablet and closes his eyes, waiting for relief.

He may or may not have fallen asleep. All he remembers is opening his eyes and seeing a couple of kids watching him. They are very young, no more than eight or nine years old, and he wonders what they are doing on their own. Probably going to the toilet together, he thinks. He offers a smile, the type that is meant to transmit a neutral nonthreatening status. The two kids, two little boys with blond hair, thick and straw-like, don't return his smile, but continue to stare at him. They have curiously flat faces, and he notices they each carry a pumpkin shaped basket, like the ones you get at Halloween to gather up your trick or treats, except these are old, woven from dirty hair and twisted branches. The pumpkin smiles are crooked, the eyes narrow slits.

'You OK, boys?' he offers, disconcerted by the crack in his voice, which makes it nowhere near as confident as he wants it to sound.

'We're OK – safe in the furrows!' they chime in unison. That feeling of unravelling returns and he thinks it is then he wakes up for real. The vestibule is empty. His heart hammers in his chest and acid squirts into his throat. *What the fuck is up with me*, he thinks.

The hiss of a sliding door breaks apart his thoughts.

It's the drunk, looking for the toilet. He spies Pete with obvious delight.

'Comfy, are we?' he scoffs. He makes a big display of shaking his head, the smirk on his face growing wider. 'You like hanging around toilets, don't you!?' His laugh is a theatrical sneer.

He fumbles with the button to open the toilet door and Pete is on his feet. He plants a foot into the small of the man's back, pushing him inside, following him in with frightening speed. Pete hits the 'lock' button and the door clicks shut. The drunk man howls in anger. He's on his knees on a piss-soaked floor. Pete hooks an arm around his neck, lifting him off his feet. He hangs about two inches off the ground and Pete presses his thumb into his windpipe. The man struggles, but with waning enthusiasm. Air whistles thinly through his nose and after a moment his eyes roll back white, doubling his weight in Pete's arms. He manoeuvres the man onto a cracked toilet seat, propping him against the wall.

Pete assesses his problem. As he thinks he reaches forward and pinches the man's nostrils shut. At the same time, he places his other hand firmly over his mouth. An electric current seems to run through him making his feet rattle on the floor. Pete counts to ten softly in his head as he watches a bruise creep up the inside of his collar, staining the man's neck. He knows how long it takes to leave this piece of shit with irreparable brain damage or leave him dead.

The moment that would signal the former approaches, and Pete toys with the idea, rolling it around in his head, seeing if it finds a landing place. He thinks of Dave and his veiled threat. The importance of being Dawn.

Fuck it, he thinks. He lets go and the man slumps to one side, his head finding a resting place on the stainless-steel sink that juts out from the wall. He groans, and spittle rolls down his chin. He's pissed himself. The stain at his crotch spreads downwards, mapping an undiscovered continent on his suit trousers.

He won't be bothering any passengers for a while. That, thinks Pete, is a good thing. He examines the locking system on the automatic door. There is an old out-of-order sign on the floor. He nods to himself.

****

The train pulls into Moreton-in-Marsh at 16.36, around thirty-five minutes behind schedule. The autumn sky above the station is drawing towards dark.

Pete gets off the train, carried along within a crowd of grey-haired old ladies. They chatter excitedly, like birds on a wire, as he walks with them along the platform and joins a queue that snakes up to the ticket barriers.

Through a brightly lit window, he observes a train guard knocking on the toilet door. He has the out-of-order sign in his hand. As the train pulls away, Pete glimpses the dishevelled figure of the drunk man being supported out of the toilet.

Pete smiles, feeling a bit better. Feeling like he'd made the right choice. He hopes the drunk will make better choices in future but suspects that won't be the case. Lessons are hard learnt.

Chapter 4

It's dark by the time Pete collects his hire car. The offices of the hire company are tucked away at the back of a small trading estate of corrugated buildings, located on the other side of the railway tracks, and well away from the chocolate box vista that welcomed visitors to Moreton-in-Marsh, the so-called gateway to the Cotswolds.

An uninterested middle-aged woman pushes keys across a chipped counter and points vaguely in the direction of the carpark, where he finds his nondescript Audi. He stows his rucksack in the boot, pulls out his phone and enters a postcode into Google maps. It says his destination is a fifty-minute drive away. The place is a hamlet called Little Baddington.

Dave provided him with a link to a website that allowed him to book a cottage on the Baddington Estate. The website was sparse, but it delivered what was required. A destination that was out of the way, quiet, and nowhere near London. The cottage had been available for six weeks and he'd made the booking, confirming he'd done so with Dave, who'd responded with a bland 'OK'.

He presses the Audi's start button, the dashboard illuminates, and he's immediately greeted by a red petrol warning light. Pete sighs. The hire car is meant to come with half a tank in it. The satnav pops up a well-meaning message asking him if he wants directions to the nearest petrol station. Pete looks across the car park to the office, but the lights have been switched off. The bored woman has presumably shut up shop and gone home, but he wanders over and checks anyway. He rattles the door, which is locked. There is no sign of the woman, or anyone else for that matter, a fact Pete finds odd given it is only 6pm, but he's grown used to London, and its twenty-four-hour life. Things work differently out in the sticks, he reminds himself.

Moreton-in-Marsh is as close to a metropolis as he's going to get around these parts, and is his best bet to fill up before he heads out into the countryside, where he might be miles away from any petrol station. Little Baddington is no more than a dot on the map, a tiny hamlet, nestled alongside a river and some ancient woodlands that bracket the estate. He knows it has a pub with some rooms, because he's reserved one for a couple of nights, but little else. He has six weeks to learn whatever else there is to know. The thought of all that time, and the absence of things to do with it, is a pleasant one.

Pete wanders back to his car. He takes a breath of cool autumnal air and reminds himself that the purpose of his trip is to relax, to get himself straight again. Getting wound up at the first mishap is not the way to start. The moon is rising above the rooftops of Moreton-in-Marsh, and he contents himself with thoughts of a welcoming fire and a nice pint in the pub when he arrives.

****

The roads narrow as Little Baddington draws closer on the illuminated satnav map. The signal on Pete's phone is stuttering, the usual definition of Google maps giving way to a blocky patchwork of dull greens and browns. He is entering single-track territory now, where tall hedgerows lean in greedily over broken asphalt, grasping at the sides of the hire car with sticky fingers. It is slightly disconcerting how quickly civilisation has dissolved on his journey, and he finds himself hankering for some streetlights. The halo provided by the car's headlights offer him a narrow window through the night and he begrudgingly admits he's a little spooked.

He comes to an incline, and for a moment he welcomes a release from the claustrophobic confines of the lane. There is a view of the road winding down into a valley which, when lit by the harvest moon, looks like a woven quilt of English countryside, albeit painted in ephemeral black and white tones. The bright moon picks out the dotted shapes of livestock in distant fields. Pete brings the car to a slow halt. The satnav says his destination is about fifteen minutes away. He grimaces, unhappy with the way the hair is now rising on his neck. He drops the window with a push of a button and allows the cool air to play over his face. He hears the distant bleat of an animal, carried on a wind that creeps up the valley and through the leaves in the trees. His instincts are telling him something is wrong, and whilst he has learned to trust them unquestioningly over the course of his career, he is bemused by the singular lack of obvious threat.

Pete turns on the car radio, in the hope that some background music or inane DJ chatter will calm his nerves and maybe still that voice in his head that is telling him, quietly and calmly, that he is in danger. Instead, all he gets is a burst of static, like fingernails on a chalkboard, followed by stuttering fragments of garbled conversation. He picks out bits of what sounds like a sermon of some sort, but is so broken into pieces, its meaning is turned into mess.

He flicks it off, irritated by his own skittishness, and eases the car forward, driving over the crest of the hill, where he is consumed once again by high-sided hedgerows. They start to fragment into wooded forest as the lane weaves downwards and begins to widen. The fields he spotted earlier start to reveal themselves in gaps between the trees, and his headlights illuminate a myriad of pinprick reflections. He slows the car again, dropping his window, and hears the soft bleat of animals, sheep or goats, he thinks, but in numbers he can't quite process. The fields are full of them, their odd rectangular-shaped eyes lighting up in the headlights. The restless bleating peters out and they stand silently, seemingly in muted judgement of his passage.

There's a sign up ahead, almost devoured by a hedgerow, but playing peek-a-boo with his headlights.

'*Little Baddington*', it says, and beneath it, '*Forever Restful in the Furrows.*'

He's arrived.

****

As Pete drives past the sign, the greedy hedgerows bordering the road are slowly subdued. They drop to a uniform height, and the moonlight reveals white scars where they have been tamed by a chainsaw. He's able to catch glimpses of electric light burning in the window of a property nestled between trees, and can't help but feel a sneaking sense of relief. He's all for a bit of solitude, but for a moment or two it'd felt like he was driving off the edge of the known world.

A crossroads appears. To his left Pete sees the looming presence of an enormous church. Far larger than he expected for such a small place. Its steeple races upwards and pierces the night sky, reflecting moonlight onto a walled graveyard that surrounds it. Its entrance is shrouded by dense yew trees, illuminated by a single Victorian lamppost. The tree's branches are liberally decorated with small hanging shapes, swaying from side to side in the breezes that inhabit the night, casting dancing shadows across the path by the road.

To his right, the road follows the edge of a village green. He sees a maypole at its centre, looking forlorn and careworn in the autumn night. The green meanders its way towards a row of tubby little cottages. A few scattered windows are illuminated, revealing occupation, but otherwise the village appears deserted.

The satnav says his destination, a pub called The Yew Tree, is up the road to the right, not more than a hundred metres past the row of cottages. Habit flicks the indicator, and the village green is bathed in intermittent orange. It takes only a minute before the crunch of gravel under his tyres signifies his arrival. He parks at the rear of the pub alongside the one other vehicle, a battered green Land Rover; otherwise it is empty.

Pete decides to leave his rucksack in the car. He'll come back for it later, his priority is a nice cool pint and something to eat. It's been a long day. He walks around to the front entrance, admiring the freshly painted façade, which is illuminated by the glow of hidden lamps that throw soft light up against the brickwork. The name of the pub, The Yew Tree, has been stencilled onto fresh paintwork. It looks every inch as nice as it did on the website when he made his booking. He reaches the front door and pushes it open, already anticipating a warm fire and equally warm welcome.

The pub is empty. There is a fire in an inglenook to the right of a bar which runs along the far wall, but its flickering warmth seems to be fighting a losing battle with the emptiness of the place. There are several tables, all neatly set up for dinner, but they look unwanted, like a stage set never to be occupied.

Pete looks around for something that might be used to call for service. Everything looks fresh, new, spotless even, but at the same time he can't help thinking that it might as well be shrouded in dust and cobwebs, like Miss Havisham's place in *Great Expectations*.

He peers over the bar and hears muted voices coming from behind a door at the far end. Above it is an old sign, battered, dirty and out of keeping with the general Farrow & Ball textures that have been imprinted on the rest of the place. It says, 'Local Bar'.

Pete's familiar with the concept, the corner of every drinking establishment that is forever frozen in time for the benefit of a very specific type of patron. The local. The people who belong.

Pete pushes the door open and in doing so slices in two the muted conversation that is taking place, so completely he can almost hear a broken sentence shattering onto the tiled floor. The local bar is very different to the room he's just left. It's currently occupied by three men, each perched on a stool alongside a small oval bar. The room has been redecorated with the same Farrow & Ball colour scheme as the dining room, but the edges of it are tarnished, some of it deliberately so judging by the dirty handprints up the wall and scuff marks up the wood-panelled frontage, as if vandalised by a belligerent child.

The three occupants turn and give him an appraising look, like crows on a wire. They are a motley crew who, judging by their mud-stained attire, work on the land, farmers, or possibly gamekeepers. Pete's untroubled by their attention. Hard stares from hard men are of little consequence to him. 'Evening, gents,' he says. 'I'm looking for the owners?'

'Owners?!' the older of them snorts. 'Is that what they are then?' He wears a flattened oil cloth hat that sits just above his ears and looks as though it has been there for a generation. His face is heavily lined with dirt, and the hair that squirts out from under the hat is dirty grey. He shares mean-spirited laughter with his companions.

A young man emerges from behind the bar. He has long brown hair that's tied into a small knot high up on the back of his head. Pete thinks they call that style a 'man bun' and doubts it's one well received in this neck of the woods. His face is pinched and pale, tension etched into his skin. He has the look of a man who expects laughter to be at his expense.

''Ere 'e is,' says the second of the men. 'Ole handsome Harry, he's your 'Owner'….' He says it with a grin that makes a point of leaving speech marks hanging in the air.

The young man spots Pete and his face fills with relief. An escape hatch has appeared in his evening, and he's ready to leap through it, regardless of what's on the other side.

49

'Ah, it must be Mr Collins, perfect, you found us!' he exclaims. Pete nods. Collins is the name he used on the booking.

'I'm so sorry, have you been waiting long? I hope not. I was changing a barrel, the guys, well, they get through it...' he chuckles nervously, searching the room for affirmation that doesn't come. The three men say nothing.

'Well, I better help Mr Collins settle in, you OK for now, Noah, John..?' he says, his voice full of hopeful bonhomie. He can't get out from behind that narrow bar quickly enough. 'Come back through to the restaurant,' he says. 'We've been expecting you. Hope your journey was OK, bit of a trek down from London, I'll bet.' *He's babbling*, thinks Pete. 'We're a little out of the way, but well worth the effort I think you'll find.'

The door to the local bar shuts behind them, and he seems to calm down a little, as if he's back on home turf. 'My name's Craig,' he says, holding out a hand which Pete accepts. It is warm, soft and a little sweaty. 'How's London doing? We used to live out Hampstead way, before, well, before we moved down here.' He looks wistful and his voice trails off.

Pete ignores the question. 'You've got a nice place,' he says, 'You had it long?'

'Long? No, not really,' says Craig. 'Bought it about twelve months ago now, spent the first six months tearing it down and the next six building it back up again, you know how it is.' Pete nods noncommittally. 'It was a bit of a wreck, but we saw it come up for auction and well, you know, fell in love with the place. London was horrid during the pandemic, all that madness, and moving here, getting away from it all, seemed like a great idea.'

'I'll bet,' says Pete, 'And was it? A great idea?'

Craig looks wistfully around the empty bar/restaurant. 'It's been harder than we expected. Little Baddington is a bit more off the beaten track than we realised. Everyone is...' he pauses, chewing over his words. 'Nice,' he says, but as if he is trying to convince himself. 'But I don't know, it takes a while to settle in, doesn't it. Lots of the folks around here have never been anywhere else, it's that type of place, you know. Takes a while for them to let you in, if you get my meaning.'

Pete nods. He gets the meaning. He takes in Craig's neat hair bun and his well-pressed shirt. He looks as if he belongs in Hampstead, not in Little Baddington, and certainly not in the company of the men who frequent the local bar.

'Well you can take your pick of a table,' he says with a desperate laugh. 'But can I get you a drink first? You must be thirsty. I can recommend the Fat Ferret, it's brewed in Moreton-in-Marsh, lovely stuff, 100% organic, really hoppy, you know.' Pete can sense Craig's enthusiasm, but has little patience for real ale, any more than he has patience for wine buffs or foodies of any sort. The ability to source locally, to eat organic, is the type of privilege that gets under his skin, even when it's well intentioned, tone deaf as it is to the problems of the many, rather than the passions of the few.

'Sounds great,' says Pete.

Craig sets to work locating a glass. It has a grinning ferret stencilled onto its side and is a strange shape. He winces at the sight of it, but ruefully acknowledges the beer that Craig pumps into it looks a hundred times more appetising than the flat muck he'd drunk with Dave back in Tower Hamlets.

'So where are you from, Mr Collins? London? You work up there? What brings you to Little Baddington?'

'It's Pete, and yes, I live up town. Just here to get some fresh air, relax...'

'Well there's no shortage of that. In fact it's about all there is to do around here, breathe the air and relax...' says Craig. He hands Pete his pint.

'You're staying with us two nights?'

'Yep, I've booked a cottage on the estate. Going to use it as a base, to explore, you know. They said I can collect the key Monday morning.'

'Great idea. There's actually loads to see and do around here, well not around here, but you know around. Really popular these days, the Cotswolds, especially in the summer. Lots of people from town have holiday homes down here. In the summer it's buzzing, at least most of it is, the buzz hasn't quite found Little Baddington yet, but you know, we're working on it!'

'Good for you. Like I say, it's a lovely place you've got here. I'm sure it'll fill up, in time.'

'Yeah, we hope so.' Craig sighs. 'Are you hungry? The kitchen's open, we have almost everything on the menu. Happy to rustle something up for you.' He hands Pete a piece of paper. It's got that rich quality to it, and the type face is all Hampstead, as are the dishes offered. Pete's not sure there is a lot of call amongst the locals for braised monkfish cheeks, certainly not at £35.

'Some food would be really good, thanks,' says Pete. He has a quick glance and selects 'Baddington Stew'.

'Excellent choice, you see it's goat meat, sometimes that puts people off, but it's amazing. Really rich flavour, fatty, so underrated. A local speciality in fact. Goats everywhere around here, they love them!'

'That's great then...' says Pete.

Craig takes the menu back from him with enthusiasm. 'I'll let Penny know. That's my wife. She's the cook, or should I say chef, it'll be with you in no time...'

Craig exits through a door at the back of the bar. Pete hears Craig call out his order, a slightly unnecessary flourish, he thinks. He picks up his pint, takes a careful sip and wanders over to the inglenook fireplace. He hears muffled laughter from the local bar. The fire cracks and pops. It's a soothing sound and he picks a table close enough to benefit from its warmth.

Above the fireplace, the immaculate new paintwork is sullied by the ghost of a symbol which seems to have stubbornly resisted the redecoration. It looks old, a round circle with two horn-like appendages on top, and a cross immediately underneath. He's wondering what it's meant to mean, when Craig returns from the kitchen.

'Found yourself a table then,' he says. 'Plenty to choose from, nice to be by the fire though, you can feel the change out there, can't you. Autumn is on its way, and not before time. The summer seemed to go on forever this year. I'm ready for some cooler nights...'

Pete smiles but says nothing. He takes another sip of his beer, which is really very good. The faint sound of a bell catches Craig's attention. 'Ah,' he says with nervous smile. 'The natives are getting restless. Duty calls!' He heads through to the local bar, and Pete can see him stiffen up as he goes, as if someone's rammed discomfort down his spine.

Pete is pondering the symbol, and is about to attempt a quick Google search, when the kitchen door opens. A young woman, Penny he presumes, holds the door open with her rump, as she navigates the narrow space behind the bar. In one hand is a broad white bowl, in the other a dish containing assorted vegetables, both of which steam pleasingly. She catches Pete's eye and offers a small smile. She is pretty, her dark hair tied up on her head in a blue bandana. She wears gleaming chef's whites. 'Hello,' she says. 'I'm guessing this is for you.' Her eyes sweep across empty dining tables.

The oversized bowl is set before Pete with a slight flourish. 'Looks great,' he says encouragingly.

'Thanks, hope you enjoy.' She leaves as quickly as she arrived. *Clearly not one for small talk*, thinks Pete, which is fine. His stomach growls at the smell of the stew, which looks delicious. He picks up a fork and sets about it.

The door to the local bar opens, and the three men walk through. Craig hovers behind them. The older one, was he called Noah, thinks Pete, stops halfway across the room and takes off his cap. He bows his head in the direction of the fireplace. Pete watches as the other two follow him, offering the same reverential nod towards it. Pete's half expecting this to be some sort of wind-up, the type of thing the locals might do as a prank, but decides the act is clearly as natural to them as breathing, a habit presumably instilled over many years. They ignore him as they file out of the front door and head off into the night.

Craig offers a nervous smile. 'Funny old lot,' he says. 'They have their ways around here, you know, traditions....great, you've got your food, good, I hope?'

Pete nods. 'Very,' he says, meaning it. He's nearly finished. 'What is that anyway..?' he asks.

'What, that, er, the fireplace?'

'Not the fireplace...that,' he says, pointing his fork at the symbol.

'Ah, that. We tried to paint over it, but the bloody thing keeps coming through, doesn't matter how many coats you slap on it. Some pagan thing or another, I think. Ha!' His laugh is brittle. 'The folk in the village, they're quite an old-fashioned lot. They take all the old stuff very seriously, you'll see. Harvest Festival, All Hallows' Eve, they celebrate it all. You saw the church when you arrived? Did you see the size of the place? It's massive, you could fit the population of the village inside it about ten times over. God knows why they built such a massive one here, in the middle of nowhere...'

'Pagan, you say?' says Pete.

'Well, something like that. The goat god, Pan, whatever. I said they have loads of them around here, didn't I? Goats, I mean. They like to give it a little bow, when passing. They all do. Takes a bit of getting used to. I'm not converted yet, but maybe once we've lived here a bit longer, we'll sign up as well! Not much use for Pan back in London, but I suppose he's a bit more relevant here. They even got a statue of a bloody goat in the church, if you can believe it...'

Pete nods; he glances at his bowl, and for a moment he sees movement in the dark residue of the stew, squirming movement. His stomach rolls softly, the stew no longer looking as appetising as it did before.

Craig is looking at him with polite interest. 'Are you OK, you've gone a little green?'

'I, no, I'm fine, just a bit of indigestion.'

'Tell me about it,' says Craig. 'Gut flora is a really big deal, you know. You look after the gut, and the gut looks after you. It's all connected, much more than anyone ever realised. I think that stuff's really important, don't you? Like the way one small things impacts another. We're all one big ecosystem, you know...'

Pete barely hears him and chances a glance at his bowl. It's not squirming anymore, and he convinces himself he imagined it, although he's quietly regretting his menu choice. That sense of danger has returned, uninvited and equally unwelcome. He feels it sitting on his shoulders, the weight constricting his breathing, inviting his heart to beat a little faster.

'Anyway, I'll take that away for you, if you're done?' says Craig. 'Can I interest you in some dessert? We have a really nice apple pie, local apples, from the orchard behind the school?'

Pete thinks about his squirming stew, the possibility he'd been busily enjoying a bowl of maggoty goat flesh, and decides against any further sustenance. The way his mind's working he figures he's liable to see something unpleasant in his pie too.

'I'm actually a bit tired. Might call it a night, if you don't mind,' says Pete. Craig looks disappointed but smiles. 'Of course. I can show you up to your room. Do you have any bags I can help you with?'

Pete shakes his head. 'Just the one,' he says. 'I'll go and grab it, I could do with a bit of fresh air.'

'Sure, OK. Well, I'll just wait here then,' says Craig.

Pete's relieved to get outside. The cool air acts as a balm, soothing troubled thoughts that he can't quite explain. He pauses for a moment, takes a deep breath and looks up to the heavens. The moon's risen to its full glory and gapes at him from the sky. He imagines it as the oblique eye of a goat, watching him. He runs a shaking hand through his hair. A good night's sleep will help, he thinks. Perhaps he's underestimated the stress he's been under, the toll that the job was taking. It was easily done, he's often thought that he bargained away a part of his soul for each one he took, and at some point, there would be a reckoning. When the last tattered fragment of his own was left, fluttering in a breeze that would eventually suck him down into hell.

He retrieves his rucksack from his car and returns to the bar. Craig greets him with puppy-dog enthusiasm.

'I'll take you up to your room? Can I take your bag?'

'No, thanks. It's fine,' says Pete.

Pete follows him up a narrow staircase that adjoins a similarly narrow landing. The floor is uneven, and the doorframes lean haphazardly, giving a fun-house aspect that adds to Pete's nausea. He's glad to get into his room, which is at the far end of the landing. He wishes Craig a hurried goodnight and shuts the door on his disappointed face.

He collapses onto a double bed. The metal frame briefly rattles against the wall, but it is soft and welcoming. He can feel some of the tension in his neck recede, and after a moment he props himself up on his elbows and has a look at his surroundings.

The room is decorated much like the bar was downstairs, a determined effort at modernisation that has paid off, but not entirely. Again, there are places where the old building has resisted progress. The ceiling above the door to the en-suite is the yellow of piss-stained sheets. In the window, hanging from the frame are a series of small figurines, twisted into shape from dirty corn stalks. They resemble a line of tiny executions, victims of an ancient hangman, swaying gently in their nooses. Considering how averse Craig says he is to the 'old ways' of Little Baddington, Pete's a little surprised he's decided to decorate his guest rooms with them.

He gets up and takes a closer look. They are truly unpleasant, with tiny screwed-up faces, each offering a scream of agony. The window offers a view down the road to the village. He sees movement. The three locals from earlier are standing on the green. They seem to be looking at him, although he can't be sure. Either way they've not headed home, and it's not clear what entertainment they've found down in the darkness.

Pete's all out of energy. He pulls the curtains shut, covering the nasty figures, and calls it a night, hoping his equilibrium will be restored with a good night's sleep.

Chapter 5

There is a honey-coloured stone cottage nestled within a copse of trees to the right of Little Baddington's church. The morning sky is still peppered with alien stars when a single light illuminates its upstairs window.

Inside, Margaret Burrell pulls a terry-towelling nightgown around herself, slides her feet into some slippers and picks her way down a steep wooden staircase. It creaks in all the usual places, the familiar symphony that greets her every day, as comforting as the soft hum of prayer that escapes her lips as she fills a kettle in the tiny kitchen.

Margaret pulls open curtains that cover a window above her sink and welcomes the first light of dawn that crests the horizon. After a moment, sunlight breaks through the trees, fractured beams of light in a morning mist that fill her soul with solid certainty of God's wondrous creation.

Margaret is the long-serving custodian of Little Baddington church, a role that she has embodied for more years than anyone can remember. Her grey hair is pulled back in a tight bun, pinned so firmly that it survives her night of sleep. The truth is she doesn't move much in her narrow single bed once settled. There is something vaguely corpselike about the way she lies, with her arms folded primly across her flat chest, not that anyone has ever witnessed the fact. She's a spinster and perfectly happy with that arrangement.

She is not a universally popular individual in the village, but that is, she thinks, not an unexpected outcome, nor one that she feels is necessarily a reflection of her own personal characteristics. In her experience, those endowed with positions of power and influence inevitably attract the ire of less favoured folk. And her role is a position of great power in the village, never more so in fact.

Father Caleb, who she still thinks of as the 'new vicar' even if it's over five years since he took over from her own dear Father (Thomas), relies upon her, he trusts her. They work together in all aspects of the church, maintaining the integrity of this wonderful community, this little slice of grace that they are blessed to call home.

Her brow furrows, and a look of delicate spite blooms on her face. There are, she thinks, a few too many folks in the village that need to realise that it isn't enough to simply enjoy the fruit. Some of them need to do much more to tend the tree whence it came. These days people seemed to think just turning up at church every Sunday, hollering a few hymns and tossing a few pounds on the plate would suffice. It wouldn't. It demanded sacrifice, of the spiritual variety of course, and she hankers for days when what is required will need to be more explicit. She shivers at the thought, provoking a memory of the last time, those hushed village meetings. The fear. Quite intoxicating!

The kettle whistles. It is time for a cup of tea. Then she will wash her face in the sink upstairs, dress, and attend to her first job of the day. The first job of every day in fact. She will open the church, light the candles, fire up the boiler so its ambient temperature is raised from freezing to tolerable, and then take time for silent prayer, before Father Caleb joins her.

She is officially allowed Mondays off but chooses not to do so. What would she do with the free time anyway? The devil makes work for idle hands, does he not, she muses. She washes her cup, puts it back in its place on the shelf and heads back upstairs.

****

The air outside is sharp with a promise of frost. The days when the hedgerow that runs alongside her house will be festooned with white, when spiderwebs will be transformed into icy decorations, are not far away, thinks Margaret, as she crunches along the pea shingle path that will take her to the entrance of the churchyard. Her little cottage is grace and favour, courtesy of the parish council. It, like her, belongs to the Lord. Her breath plumes in front of her, a pleasing steam engine chugging dutifully along well-worn tracks. The iron key to the church door sits coldly in her fist. It is strung onto a piece of rope that she thinks might be as old as she is.

The walk to the church is short, no more than three minutes door to door. Its door is heavy, rattling as loudly as if trying to wake the village from slumber, and part of Margaret enjoys the way it disturbs the silence. The Lord's work requires activity, not idleness, she thinks. If she's able to break free of her bed at this hour, she fails to see why others cannot also, although she respectfully excludes Father Caleb from that admonishment. He's entitled to his rest, tireless as he is in supporting her and the community.

The church is encased in darkness, and she flicks up the bank of switches that provide illumination. The bulbs are old and sickly, and the shadows only make a partial retreat. The boiler room is in the back of the church, located via a small office that she used to use for clerical work. Thankfully she's convinced Father Caleb to change some things and she doesn't need to do as much paperwork as she used to.

Once the boiler is lit, Margaret sets about her next task. It's a personal favourite.

She carefully sets trap the night before, just before lights out. The building is old and close to the fields. Years of experience have taught her the best spots, and most mornings deliver a prize. Today is no exception. The first trap she checks, the one just inside the vestibule, is snapped shut. The 'humane' traps are a blessing. Keeping God's little creations safe and well, but also ensuring the hungry little beggars can't chew through the wires and cause untold damage to the fabric of the church. It's a war of attrition, but one she's happy to maintain as a functional stalemate. The countryside's supply of mice and rodents is seemingly endless.

Margaret gives the plastic tube a little shake and feels the pleasing shift of weight that confirms she has a captive. She checks the cap is secure before placing it into the pocket of her overcoat (which she hasn't removed yet, it will be a good hour before the boiler has done its work and taken the chill out of the air). She checks the other traps, but these prove less successful, and she's faintly disappointed. She wonders if switching to cheese from peanut butter will improve results. One mouse is slim pickings, and possibly not enough for her other important task of the morning.

No matter, she thinks. The Lord provides what the Lord feels is required, and it is not for her to question his infinite wisdom.

Margaret fishes a box of matches out of her other pocket. She scrapes it across a stone altar that stands guard at the front of the church. The smell of sulphur that accompanies the burst of flame is pleasing, and apt, she thinks with a nervous giggle. For a moment she looks a little like a schoolgirl caught doing something forbidden. That expression on her face is an unlikely and not entirely pleasant combination. She lights the candles that sit either side of a wide metal dish, before blowing out the match and putting its blackened stub in her pocket.

She hums tunelessly as she fishes out first the mousetrap and then a small pocketknife from her pocket. Above the altar, daylight is starting to make its presence known, transforming the stained-glass window into a rainbow of colour. She feels only peace, as she extracts the mouse from its plastic tube, pulling it out by the tail and wrapping it gently within her fist. She shushes it indulgently. It wriggles furiously before falling still. Her other hand opens the pocketknife. She can easily do it one-handed, the movement is metronomic, as is her heartbeat, which she fancies is now in time with that of her furry captive.

Margaret pushes the blade of the knife through the mouse's skull with a soft sigh of satisfaction. Blood, a vibrant red, runs over her fist and onto a plate below. She squeezes the mouse's body with all her strength, feeling tiny bones pulp, wringing out every last drop of its precious sustenance. She smiles. A blood sacrifice is really the only way to start a day. The only welcome appropriate in the presence of her Lord.

He who walks in the furrows, all praise be....

****

Pete wakes early and decides to head out for a run.

It's part of his normal routine, and one he is loath to depart from. The run is care and maintenance, of body and mind. He can hear that someone else is up and about despite the early hour, maybe Craig, maybe Penny, but Pete manages to slip out of the front door into a morning mist without having to make any small talk, which is a relief.

The air is crisp, ripe with the first blast of autumn, and carries the smell that foreshadows the winter to come. So far this year the trees have resisted the seasons, but now their leaves, encouraged to linger by warm days, can sense the turning air and its light fingers that will guide them into golden hues before they're drowned in decay.

He did a bit of research before he arrived, and his watch has been programmed with a 10K run that'll take him out of the village and onto footpaths that weave along the estate. It looked like a good chance to familiarise himself with his surroundings, a habit that is engrained in him, but the mist that now blankets the village means his views might be limited.

He runs down the road he drove up the night before, passing the village green on his right, his body swiftly falling into familiar rhythm, his footfall metronomic, his heartbeat the same. The maypole is no longer visible, shrouded by mist, and the church beyond it is reduced to a dark smudge. His watch commands him to take a right, and he spots the start of a footpath that should take him over some fields behind the church. It's narrow, bordered by bramble hedgerows and nettles that lean in greedily. He shimmies past, keen to avoid their acid touch against his bare legs.

About 200 metres along, the path meets a kissing gate, old and worn. The pathway has deteriorated and mud sucks at Pete's trainers. He pushes through a gap in the hedgerow and finds himself in a vast field. The mist offers only a limited view of its scale, but there is an aching sense of space that is disorientating. Looking at his watch, he can see the footpath is meant to cross this field on a diagonal. That far side is lost to the mist, which means he's going to have to trust his watch. The soil is recently ploughed and heavy with clay. He fears for his ankles but is committed now. He's warmed up nicely and that isn't a feeling you want to waste.

The mist closes in around him, and but for the reassuring pulse of his watch, Pete could be anywhere in space and time.

Focused as he is on not making a misstep and turning an ankle, Pete doesn't register the shapes that appear ahead of him and to his right. His eyes are on the ground ahead of his feet, judging the placement of each, the simple task focusing him in that peculiarly delightful way familiar to all runners.

His nerves trigger a warning, something primal, and within a second, he's back in the moment. He freezes. There is a person, or something like a person, standing in the mist ahead of him. It stands, arms outstretched, as if crucified. It wears a dirty brown raincoat, old and torn, its edges shredded. The eddying pools of mist make it difficult to tell how far away it is, or indeed what it is. It blurs in and out of vision as the mist eddies in the gentle morning breeze. Each time it reappears it seems to have shifted position, moving subtly to the left and then the right. But closer each time.

Pete isn't a superstitious person, he has no experience of or interest in the paranormal, or any of the stuff he considers mindless mumbo-jumbo, but he's learnt to believe what he sees and feels in any given moment. That way he deals with whatever's happening without the baggage of a rational brain.

The figure, for that is what it is, has a misshapen head, flattened into stooped shoulders. Crescent eye slits and a jagged mouth complete a Jack-o-Lantern effect, but this head is a diseased brackish brown, rather than bright orange.

The mist swirls again and the scarecrow drops out of sight. Pete's every instinct screams that when it reappears it will be closer still, maybe close enough to touch.

He runs.

The uneven ground is a challenge, but he rises to it. He runs without thought of what might follow him, how close it might be, whether it will close a fungal hand onto a shoulder. He runs with high strides, eating up the ground, relying on the steady pulse of his watch to keep him on track. Eventually a dark line materialises out of the mist, tightening in form, becoming a hedgerow. In the corner is another kissing gate.

He chances a look over his shoulder, and sees only eddying pools of mist, displaced by his wake. The touch of the cold metal gate, its reassuring solidity, allows him to reconnect with reality. His breathing slows as he scans the edges of the mist for any sign of movement. This isn't what he's come out of London for.

****

Pete dutifully follows his GPS back to the village. He is grateful for it, as the so-called footpath has been more or less invisible for the duration of his run, which he's prudently trimmed in length. He's plotted a different route through the mist back to the village. One that avoids open fields.

It's clear no-one in Little Baddington is making any use of the tangle of footpaths that weave across the estate. It's almost as if they're deliberately unkempt. By the time he's circled back to the village via a small wood the path is all but impassable, fractured by fallen trees and swallowed by hungry brambles. Whoever owns Baddington Estate shows little interest in attracting ramblers, or anyone else for that matter.

Pete caught a glimpse of an imposing house just before the woodlands, after he'd run adjacent to a stone wall for at least a mile. He assumes it's where Lord Baddington lives. He'd come across a fairly neutral Wikipedia page about him when he did a search, after he booked his cottage. It described another toff, living well and growing old off the back of inherited (and probably stolen) wealth.

He finds himself at the boundary of Little Baddington and spots the formidable spire of the church. He allows himself to slow his run to a walk. He wonders when he got flighty enough to be spooked by a scarecrow in a field. The church yard is accessed via an old wooden porch. It's been swallowed up by a twisted canopy of ancient yew trees that bind together in a desperate lovers' embrace, creating a dark green tunnel up to the front door of the church.

The path beneath Pete's feet is littered with yew needles that scrunch softly underfoot as he approaches the vestibule. The heavy wooden door beyond opens with a clunk of the latch, and a man steps out from the darkness of the church. He is young, thickset with a shaven head. If it wasn't for the dog collar around his neck, he'd look as if he could work the door of any number of clubs/bars in London. He smiles, revealing a mouthful of white teeth. He's the opposite of what Pete would come up with if asked to visualise a vicar in a place like Little Baddington.

'Good morning!' he calls, raising a meaty hand in greeting. 'A fine way to start the day.' He places his hands on his hips and takes in Pete's running kit. 'Very noble! I myself have only just risen. You shame me with your dedication!' He smiles more broadly and steps beneath the canopy of the yew trees and into shadow. His voice is crisp, with only the faintest whiff of the accent Pete associates with the area.

'Are you visiting perhaps? Forgive me, I don't recognise you. Perhaps you stay at our lovely pub?'

Pete nods. 'Got it in one.'

'Wonderful! Then you've met Craig and the delightful Penny. Newcomers to our community, but already part of the furniture. They've settled in so well...' He claps his hands together and rubs them enthusiastically. 'Very cold this morning, misty too, must have been tricky finding your way around out there, or do you have a good sense of direction?'

'Not really, I just have this,' says Pete, holding up his watch.

'Ah, of course. Modernity has a solution for everything, doesn't it. A shortcut to a skill that was once valued. I never know whether to celebrate that or curse it. Ha! I must be getting old...'

'You don't look old,' says Pete. He's still trying to get his head around this youthful pastor amidst the creaky backdrop of Little Baddington. It just doesn't fit. 'Have you worked here long?' asks Pete, wondering if he's been parachuted in recently, maybe from some tough inner city.

'Over five years, but it feels like forever. I grew up in a village near Moreton but heard about this place, so when my predecessor passed, may the Lord rest his soul delicately amidst the furrows, it seemed only right I should try and follow his good work in the community.' He looks around, his eyes shining. 'I love it here! It is a truly a wonder of creation. So, how long are you staying with us? The pub is very comfortable, but perhaps not for a prolonged stay?'

'I've rented a cottage on the estate, for six weeks. I can move in on Monday, but I wanted to get away, and, well, here I am...'

'Indeed you are.' His smile broadens, a shark's grin, thinks Pete, out of nowhere. 'My name is Caleb, Father Caleb if we are going to be formal, but no need for that. And who are you?'

'My name is Pete, Pete Collins...' He offers a hand, which Caleb declines to take. He peers at Pete closely.

'Oh, it's Pete at the moment, is it?' he says, that shark's grin broadening still further. 'Very good.'

There is a knowing implication in Caleb's smile that he finds unnerving. He flounders for a second and then Caleb takes his hand and gives it a friendly shake. 'It's wonderful to have you here. Six weeks! That is truly time to relax and settle into the peaceful tick of life here in Little Baddington.

I don't think you will want to leave!' Caleb laughs, and Pete finds himself smiling in return, as the feeling of unease scatters. *Christ, I'm on edge*, he thinks.

'Come, let me walk you to your lodgings,' says Caleb. 'I'm heading up that way. Got to collect something for tomorrow's sermon, which you're very welcome to join if you'd like?'

Pete smiles apologetically. 'I'm not really the religious type, you know, but thanks all the same.'

Caleb nods, untroubled. 'Of course, no pressure at all. The church's door is always unlocked, but that doesn't mean you are under any obligation to push on it! Just to say, you might be pleasantly surprised. I believe there's a place for everyone within the house of our Lord. All are welcome, nothing off limits. Spiritual restitution is not just reserved for the believers, you know.'

They walk up the pathway, in the embrace of the yews, when a voice calls behind them.

'Father Caleb,' it says sharply. 'Where are you going?'

Caleb spins on his heels. 'Ah, Margaret, excuse me, sorry.' He pats Pete on the arm and heads back down the path on his toes, to where a grey-faced woman stands. She glances at Pete, who offers a smile that isn't returned. Caleb exchanges some words with her, his voice low and beyond Pete's ability to eavesdrop. The woman, Margaret, radiates impatience. Pete sees her gaze flick in his direction as they speak. Her eyebrows travel up her forehead and she breaks into an unpleasant smile. Pete finds himself thinking of a nurse who'd enjoy delivering bad news.

'Sorry about that,' says Caleb. 'Margaret likes to know what's going on in the village, a new face always raises questions.' He smiles broadly.

Pete gives a small wave as they depart, which this time she returns.

'Well, I hope she's reassured?' says Pete.

Caleb barks laughter, causing Margaret's eyes to narrow. 'She'll never entirely trust an outsider. It's taken me over five years to win her over! But she has a good heart. And loves this place even more than I do. Do you know she's been custodian of the church for over fifty years, remarkable! Dedication to public life, service to a community. It's a rare thing these days, and something to be cherished.'

They reach a gate that leads onto the road that circles the village green. It's also enclosed within a wooden porch, and here, the yew trees have grown through the structure, the boughs weaving around it like ancient reptiles. Hanging from the beams that support the roof, Pete spots more of the strange corn figures that decorate his window back at the pub.

Caleb reaches up and touches one of the thick yew boughs. His hand strays down its length, as if stroking a favoured pet.

'Amazing tree, the yew, don't you think? So old, I'd guess some of these must be older than Little Baddington itself. Did you know, back in Roman times the yew tree was thought to be the guardian of the entrance to the underworld? The pagans later decided it was symbolic of everlasting life and rebirth. I'm undecided,' says Caleb with a small smile. 'But they are beautiful and will be here long after you or I have gone. There is something restful in that, a reminder of our place in the grand scheme of things.'

Caleb opens the gate, which squeaks on its hinge.

'Come, you must be growing cold,' he says. His words invite a shiver. The warmth generated by his run is dissipating and sweat is refrigerating on his back. 'The mist refuses to break this morning, but I'm sure there'll be a warm welcome for you at The Yew Tree. Penny does a very good full English, I'm told.'

They walk in companionable silence. The village remains in slumber. Pete glances at his watch, and sees it is still early, only just gone nine am. His first morning in Little Baddington has been a strange introduction. And this vicar who looks like a boxer, who is both welcoming and oddly knowing, with a gaze that winkles out secrets as efficiently as a fisherman shuck oysters, is only adding to his feeling of vague unease.

They reach the gravel drive in front of The Yew Tree. Pete can see lights on in the bar through one of the windows.

'Good to meet you, Peter,' says Caleb, reaching out and taking his hand again. His grip is strong, and Pete is again forcibly reminded of a bouncer. 'Come and see me once you've settled in on the estate. I'd be happy to show you around the area, make sure you don't miss any of the highlights, you know...'

'That's very kind, I'll take you up on that,' replies Pete. 'Can I ask you a question?'

'Of course!' says Caleb. 'Fire away!'

'I need to get some provisions before I head off to my cottage, basic stuff, milk, eggs, maybe some bread. Does the village have a shop, or will I need to head back to the mainland?'

'Haha!' says Caleb. 'Very good, yes, we are a little bit of an island here, but that's the way we like it! Of course we have a shop, it's just up the hill, near the school. It will have all you need, and more besides. Herschel's the butcher, and his wife Maria provides a small but perfectly formed bakery. If you are minded to avoid the lazy decadence of convenience food, you can find all you would ever need to make a hearty home-cooked meal. We pride ourselves on being self-sufficient here. The less we rely on the outside world the better!'

'Sounds perfect, I'll pay it a visit.'

'It is perfect. Maria's up with the lark, much like yourself. The shop remains at our service, and I can't recall a time when one of them wasn't available, although they will close briefly when it's time for church, but you would expect no less! The shop is up thataway, and I am heading thisaway, so I leave you for the morning, but hope very much to see you soon. Give my best wishes to Penny and Craig!' Caleb cries as he walks briskly away. 'Until we meet again!'

It only takes a moment before he is swallowed by the mist and Pete is left alone. He thinks Caleb is a man to whom exclamations come easy. Pete's always regarded conversational exclamations as a clear indication that meaningless words will've preceded them but decides to put his cynicism on a top shelf for now. His stomach growls, and he decides to find the shop, thinking stocking up now will mean he can get to his cottage sooner, away from Craig and the faintly depressing atmosphere of The Yew Tree.

Caleb had pointed vaguely up the road ahead, so Pete walks past the pub and continues up a short hill that is lined with cottages. The size of property increases as he walks. Little Baddington shouldn't be short of money, he thinks, all of the property has that chocolate box sheen that he associates with the countryside, or at least the bits of it that've been hijacked by wealth. That said, the village doesn't *feel* rich, not in the same way as Moreton-in-Marsh and the villages near it did, it has a curiously rough edge to it, almost out of sight but palpable, like a glamorous lady that clasps a rusty bloodstained knife behind her back. Like Craig says, the buzz hasn't quite reached here yet.

Further up the hill the mist starts to thin, and Pete can see an entrance to the school Caleb mentioned. Opposite is a shop. There is a bright red awning over its front window, with 'Village Store' printed upon it in white letters. When he pushes the door open a bell chimes pleasingly.

Chapter 6

Pete experiences 'the eye' almost immediately. It's a familiar sensation, and one that increases in both frequency and intensity when he ventures away from his home patch in East London.

Pete knows the colour of his skin, and the darkness of his eyes and hair do little to help smooth passage in this part of the world, but it is more than that. The 'eye' is a harbinger of the siren song that reminds all who hear it where they belong, establishing the invisible barriers that carefully guide the populace through the everyday. People smell difference in the way sharks sense blood in the water. It can't be disguised by fine clothes, smart watches, or even a fancy ride. It's assessed in heartbeats, where one seeks another, tests connection, familiarity, and in absence broadcasts cold reserve, if you're lucky, with a brittle politeness.

The bell that announces Pete's arrival fades, leaving behind it a block of silence that builds a wall between himself and the swiftly fading smile of a middle-aged lady who stands behind the shop counter. This must be Maria.

Pete's smile is acknowledged with a frown. She's short and slightly plump, round in the way a cosy grandma should be, but radiating hard edges instead of soft welcoming places. Her hair is brown, but is darker than her lined face would merit, and Pete thinks she must dye it. The counter she stands behind is old, made of thick battle-scarred wood.

'Morning,' says Pete.

He receives a curt nod by way of reply. A welcome without warmth, a dampened campfire with no place for him. Maria busies herself filling a display case next to the cash register with bread and pastries. Although Caleb's effusive description of the lovely Maria seems off kilter when compared to the reality, the produce in the shop looks OK to Pete. He casts a glance around the shop, spying a small stack of old wire shopping baskets. He extracts one noisily. It has a yellow plastic grip and he swings it by his side as he starts to investigate the shop with a degree of self-consciousness that irritates him.

The shop is well stocked, with an array of tinned goods as well as fresh vegetables and, to the left of the main counter, a refrigerated display case that is full of blood-red fresh meat. But it's weird. It feels as though he's stepped back in time, maybe to the 1980s. The shelves are full of brands he doesn't recognise, and the selection is limited, harking back to simpler times when no-one had heard of an avocado or needed fish sauce. He briefly entertains the idea that it's a novelty shop, maybe one that is deliberately old-fashioned, like one of those living museum things, but a glance at Maria suggests if it is she's not in on the joke.

Pete selects a few items, aware of Maria's indiscreet gaze following him around the shop. It's an experience he's used to, store detectives of one type or another have followed him on shopping trips most of his life. He's learned to ignore it.

The bell chimes again, signalling the arrival of another customer.

A woman enters the shop. She's dressed in a tweed jacket and one of those large wide-brimmed hats favoured by the country set, but is tatty and worn. Her boots looks as though they've seen service and are far away from those Hunter wellies rich folk wear that look like they'd faint if they saw a muddy puddle. 'Maria,' she says gruffly. Maria's face cracks into a smile that's reserved for privileged insiders. It's warm, friendly and transforms her into the cosy grandma she promised to be at first glance. Pete marvels at the metamorphosis, from caterpillar to butterfly.

'Morning, Elizabeth my dear,' says Maria. 'You well?' She shoots Pete another look, making it clear that as nice as it is to see her, it's not at all nice to see him.

Elizabeth notices Pete, and unlike Maria she is capable of offering a thin smile of sorts, albeit one fringed with mild disdain. It's another look that Pete, and indeed anyone in the UK who's been somewhere they don't quite 'belong', would recognise. It says 'I'll favour you with politeness, but no more than that, and politeness won't last either, so don't push it'.

She waddles over to the meat counter, peering at the product of slaughter with interest. A large man, heavyset and sporting an impressive grey mutton chop moustache and sideburns combo, appears through a doorway. He wears a long white coat and striped dark blue apron. If Pete had been asked to sketch a caricature of a butcher, then this man is he.

'Herschel!'

Herschel allows himself a constipated smile but has a face that looks unsuited to welcomes.

'Is it ready? The festivities are upon us.'

'Of course, madam,' says Herschel. He ducks behind his counter. Pete spies a large wooden block in the backroom. It's slathered with bright red blood with a large cleaver embedded in its thick surface. He pops up after a moment holding a white carrier bag. It's full of wrapped parcels and the bottom of the bag has already gathered a pool of blood. He hoists it over the counter and hands it to Elizabeth.

'*Hmph*. Appreciated, Herschel. Put that on my tab, we'll settle at month end, same as always.'

'Of course, madam,' says Herschel. Pete wonders if that's all he ever says.

Elizabeth stomps out the shop, casting Pete a suspicious look. The door tinkles recognition of her departure. Pete hears the faint growl of an engine starting, before seeing a battered car flash past the window.

He wanders over to the meat counter. Herschel looms behind it, his face monolithic. 'Hi,' says Pete as he inspects the display. 'Looks great,' he says, meaning it. The meat looks amazing, the various cuts a bright, almost iridescent red.

'Can I help you, sir?' growls Herschel. The tone of his voice suggests helping Pete is the last thing he wants to do this morning.

'I'm staying at a cottage, on the estate. Father Caleb suggested I pop in to stock up on a few bits and pieces.'

'You're staying on the estate, at Caprae Cottage?' says Maria. She pops up from behind her counter like a meerkat. Her face transforms. 'Well why didn't you say so!?' she exclaims. 'Goodness, you must think us very rude. If you're a guest of Father Caleb, then you are most welcome in our shop, isn't he, darling,' she trills. Herschel tries on a smile that is closer to a grimace, but either way Pete thinks it is an improvement on a stony face.

Maria hustles around from behind her counter. She flashes a look at Herschel that Pete can't interpret. 'You'll be wanting to stock up on a few things. Father Caleb usually puts a few items in the store cupboard for his special guests, but it's never enough. If you're lucky, you'll get a few teabags and some eggs. He's a bachelor and, well, you know what bachelors are like. No idea! Here, let me help you, we have everything you need, no reason to head out of the village if you're prepared to do a bit of cooking from scratch, and we should all be doing a bit more of that anyway. But if you're allergic to saucepans I do have a few ready meals in the freezer,' she says, with a sniff that suggests he'll be a disappointment if he goes down that route.

'I'm happy to have a crack at making my own dinner. It'll give me something to do, I'm here for a while and have nothing planned. Just time to relax, you know.'

Maria's smile broadens. Pete thinks she looks a bit like the grandma in the reverse fairy-tale. The one that ends up eating the wolf.

'Well, we've got vegetables, fresh from local farms, we've got meat that my dear Herschel butchers personally. All the usual cuts, but if you're feeling adventurous, we specialise in goat. Very underrated meat, I always say, isn't it, Hersch...'

Herschel grunts by way of a reply. Maria takes Pete by the arm and leads him over to the vegetable display. It all looks fresh and good, housed in wicker baskets that look practical rather than fake twee. They smell of soil.

'Go on then,' says Maria. 'Help yourself.'

Pete is disorientated by the sudden change in atmosphere in the shop, from sub-zero to tropical in a heartbeat. His radar is pinging loudly, telling him the version of Maria he met when he first entered the shop is closer to the real one. He suspects her true faces lurks beneath this affected hospitality. *Paranoia is a strength*, he reminds himself. *Embrace it.*

'How long are you staying with us then?'

'A few weeks,' says Pete. 'Move in tomorrow. Been staying at The Yew Inn. Nice place.'

Maria's expression experiences a minor avalanche. 'Oh, well, yes, I suppose it is. They try hard, but you know, it's difficult to make a business work in a small village. We offered Craig our services, our produce, but he, well, he had ideas of his own...' Her mouth purses, as if she's tasted something bad.

'It was pretty quiet in there last night. I hope it works out for them. A busy pub is a part of the community, right?'

'That's a shame,' says Maria, although her eyes scream the opposite. 'But yes, community. Very important,' she finishes. Her eyes take on a faintly evangelical sheen. Even old Herschel is nodding along, like one of those plastic dogs that sit on the parcel shelf of a car.

Pete gathers a few items from the shelves. He won't know quite what he picked up until later, his hands move at random. Maria watches him with bright interest, like a robin eying up a busy gardener. He finds himself in front of Herschel's counter once again, and points at cuts of meat that now make him feel faintly queasy. They don't look as appetising as they did before. The blood that pools in the metal display trays looks darker, almost spoiled. Herschel gathers up his selected cuts without putting on the little blue rubber gloves that poke up out of a box on the counter, like spring bulbs. He wipes his hands on his apron, leaving executioner smears on the cloth. Pete queasily eyes the bag that he hands over the counter. He can see himself dropping it in a bin at the first opportunity.

He takes his basket to Maria, who's returned to her spot behind the cash register. She starts to ring up his purchases. The till is ancient, and she bashes away on its keys enthusiastically, like a demented organ player. 'Some bread, perhaps?' she ventures. 'Father Caleb might have put some in your welcome bundle but I wouldn't want to say for sure...'

'Ok, yes, that'd be good,' says Pete, who's now keen to get out of this shop and put the most recent in a line of frankly odd Little Baddington interactions behind him. His brain is flashing questions at him – since when was he a guest of Father Caleb? he thinks. The man had made no mention of owning the cottage he has rented. It was just the estate. Perhaps he's a custodian of it, or something?

'That'll be £67.48 pence,' says Maria. 'I've thrown the bread in for free, given you're a special guest and all.' She gives him a sly smile.

Pete produces his watch. 'Apple Pay?' he asks hopefully.

'Oh, no. I'm afraid we don't have that here,' says Maria. 'It's cash or cheque. We looked into getting one of those card readers but there awfully expensive. Herschel says they just let bankers skim off the top anyway.' Her eyes narrow. 'Bloody banks. Can't trust them. Trust your own, that's what we say around here and we're right.' She shakes her head. 'What are we going to do about this then?' she says.

'I can see if Craig will do me some cash back at the pub. He's got a payment machine, should work,' says Pete.

'Oh does he now! Well, he's from up your way and I suppose he knows all about that fancy stuff doesn't he. That's fine,' she says briskly. 'I'll assume you're good for it. You can take the shopping and come back later to pay. You wouldn't get that type of service in London, would you...?'

'You wouldn't,' says Pete. 'I'll be back before I head off. And thank you, you've both been very helpful...'

'You'll enjoy the cottage. It's very remote. Very private. No-one will even know you are there.' Maria manages a smile.

Chapter 7

Pete does his best to sneak into the pub and tiptoe to his room, but it seems Craig's been lying in waiting, materialising from behind the bar like a depressed jack-in-the-box.

He does his best to look pleased to see him, but it's not easy. There's something about Craig's demeanour that places him in a corner of his subconscious alongside Eeyore, Droopy and other hangdog characters from his childhood. Perhaps uncharitably, he has no desire to be an emotional sounding board for a Hampstead refugee.

'I see you've met Caleb? And been to the shop?' says Craig. He nods first in the direction of the window and then at the bag in Pete's hand. 'A busy morning!'

Pete feels a trickle of annoyance which must've shown on his face as Craig is quickly on the defensive. 'Not that I've been watching you, I was up early too, happened to hear you go out and, well, then I saw you and Caleb heading up the road. It's good that you've met some of the locals. Settling in already!'

Pete reminds himself that he needs to tap Craig up for some cash to settle his debt with Maria. Dealing with that promptly feels like a good idea. He has a brief vision of Herschel turning up at his door, meat cleaver in hand. 'Went out for a run and ended up being bumping into Caleb, Father Caleb I mean. He introduced me to the neighbours. And now I've got a bag of food. You got anywhere I can store this?' he asks, holding up his grocery bag. 'I'm also going to need to ask you a favour. I've got no cash and the store's pretty old-fashioned, so this is all on credit at the moment. I got the impression that Maria's line of credit is time limited. Can you do me some cashback so I can settle up before she sets Herschel on me?'

'Ha! Of course, yes, I'll put that in our fridge and don't worry about the cash. We have a bit on site despite how quiet we are. Maria and Herschel, yes, a funny pair. You wouldn't to fall out with him, that's for sure.'

Craig takes his bag of shopping, and Pete feels a moment's hesitation. He doesn't like owing people. He thinks favours have a habit of becoming spiteful little things, swelling in size and importance, and eventually growing teeth.

'Look, can I fix you some breakfast? I'm allowed to rattle the pans when it comes to the bacon and eggs, Penny trusts me with that.' Craig forces out a laugh that clatters to the floor like broken crockery.

'Sure,' he says. 'That'd be good. Caleb said you did a great breakfast...'

'Did he?!' says Craig, hope bringing colour back to his cheeks. 'Well that's great, I mean, that's progress, right?'

'I'll just freshen up. Bit sweaty from my run.'

'Yes, sure, I'll get to work. Full English right? All the trimmings, coming right up!' Craig hustles through the bar and into the kitchen, and Pete escapes up to his room.

****

The shower in Pete's room grinds into life, the pipes rattling before spitting out a tepid flow that he does his best to work with. He's doesn't linger, dresses quickly and is soon back downstairs. He's hungry now, the run has laid foundations for appetite, and the thought of a cooked breakfast is a good one.

Craig's absent, although he can hear the rattle of pans through the door into the kitchen. Pete sits by a window, picking a table up against an old cast iron radiator, which he hopes will offer some heat. The shower was refreshing, but has left him slightly chilled, and he shudders. The windowsill is decorated with more of the twisted corn dolls, and he picks one up to examine it more closely. It has an unpleasant texture, dry but somehow fetid, as if it's throwing off microscopic layers of rancid dust that leave a greasy texture on his fingers. He puts it back down and wipes his hands on his trousers.

'Hope you're OK with coffee?' says Craig. 'I took a guess, but I can get you a pot of tea if you prefer?'

'No, coffee's good. Thanks,' says Pete.

Craig lingers by the table. 'You've seen Penny's little decorations then? She's put them up everywhere. They make them at the church, part of the Harvest Festival, she says.'

He sees the look on Pete's face and continues. 'Yeah, not quite what you'd expect, but I'm told Caleb, Margaret, well they really like the traditions. Doesn't make any sense to me.'

'I guess,' says Pete, hoping he'll be left in peace to enjoy his breakfast.

'Church isn't my thing. Never went as a kid, did you? Mum and Dad didn't buy into all that stuff. Dad hated it, church, God, kind of rubs off, doesn't it?' says Craig.

'It didn't sound like it was compulsory. Caleb seemed OK, open-minded.'

'Did he?' says Craig. 'Always felt like the church was a bit of a prerequisite, you know, especially if you want to belong around here. You're just passing through, probably less pressure on the conversion rate!'

'Right,' says Pete, wondering where the conversation is going.

'Penny's much more interested, especially these days. She wasn't to begin with, more like me, but I think she finds some comfort there, you know, things have been quite stressful here, bills to pay, and, you know, lots of empty tables....' Craig trails off, and his hand draws vague spiral patterns in the air. He looks through those patterns, perhaps hoping some answers lie within. 'It's been hard. Settling in, all the money going out, not a lot coming in. A lot harder than we expected, I guess. Not quite the dream we sold ourselves on. You know, we couldn't get one local contractor to work on our renovations. Not one. They were all too busy. We ended up using people from Cirencester. I thought they'd all pitch in – happy to help and all that. A community, but no such luck. You saw them, last night. The locals. I've not clicked with them yet. They tolerate me. If it wasn't for us they wouldn't even have a pub to sit in and sip their shitty lager.' Craig's face has gone quite red. He takes a breath. 'I suppose going to the church might help to integrate, but I can't do it.'

Pete thinks about the barbed comments Maria made in the shop. He suspects Craig may always find himself on the outside looking in.

'Penny's thrown her hat in,' says Craig. 'She says she's had enough of being on the outside. She's actually quite shy, you know, takes a while to get to know people. But she's gone for it with Caleb and his congregation. It's helped her. Made a few more friends. She doesn't talk about it much, not since I said I didn't want to join her. And the rest of them, the villagers, they're still off, and they were never really on in the first place.' His sigh is heavy.

'I'm sure things will get better, Craig,' says Pete, hoping a bland assurance might open up an escape hatch in the conversation, but Craig's not ready to let him go just yet.

'They need to. This place, it's…it's tearing us apart really. The pressure, the loneliness. I, I'm sorry. Not sure why I'm telling you all this, but I just need to let it out a bit, y' know. It was so nice to have someone other than one of the local yokels in last night,' he says, but not without looking fearfully over his shoulder at the Local Bar. 'That's what it was meant to be like. Me. Penny. Lots of nice folks from up town who wanted to eat great food, drink, just you know, be nice…Instead we get this. A deserted bar, empty tables, and the fucking god Pan presiding over it all from above the fireplace…'

Pete says nothing.

'I'm sorry, really sorry. You don't need to hear all this,' says Craig. After an uncomfortable minute or two of silence, Pete's preferred strategy seems to work and Craig heads back into the kitchen, leaving him in peace.

His breakfast's gone cold, but the run has ignited appetite sufficiently to finish it. He's about done, mopping up congealed egg with a piece of vinegary sourdough that he would've happily swapped for a slice of good old-fashioned rubbery white bread, when a footstep disturbs him. Pete's ready to move up a gear towards exasperation when he sees it's not Craig, but his wife Penny.

She's dressed in a plain black dress. Her legs are covered with stockings. Her hair is tied up in a neat bun. She looks very pretty, but in a strangely sad way, as if her appearance, beguiling as it is, is a curse. She looks flustered to have been spotted.

'I'm sorry to disturb you,' she says, taking a coat from a hanger by the door and wrestling her way into it.

'It's fine,' says Pete. 'No bother. Craig's in the kitchen, he's knocked me up a fine breakfast.'

Penny throws him a distracted smile that is gone as quickly as it arrived. 'That's good. I'm off out now...'

'Church, is it?' asks Pete. He's not quite sure why he asked, but the words are out of his mouth before he has time to check himself. Penny stops, one hand on the door. She gives Pete a look he can't quite fathom, somewhere between irritation and desperation.

'There's no service today, but there's always things to do. I like to keep busy.' She opens the door and heads out.

Pete watches her walk stiffly down the road. The mist is clearing and the bruised shadow of the church looms above the village. He sees one of the cottage doors open. A small lady emerges. She is also dressed in black. She hails Penny and they fall in step together.

Pete doesn't wants to stay any longer at The Yew Tree. The undercurrents here are too close to the surface, and he has no desire to get swept up in them any further. His personal experience of marriage guidance is limited to those occasions when his instructions from Dave make it clear which spouse is to be terminated and when. He prefers that crisp certainty to the amorphous mess that is human relationships. *There isn't a disagreement that exists that can't be settled quickly and neatly with a bullet*, he thinks.

Chapter 8

A snatch of information can become an earworm, ricocheting around, searching for a place to settle, somewhere it can burrow deep and find a home.

Pete's chewing over the throwaway comment Maria made that Caleb is responsible for his cottage. This comment becomes an inkblot on paper, spreading its tendrils, creating multiple crossroads, each offering a question that demands an answer. Paranoia was his travelling companion, brokering internal dialogue where none is necessarily required. But still, it bothers him. Why hadn't he mentioned that when he met him, why had he pretended he didn't know who he was, even after he'd given him his name? Why, why, why?

Pete doesn't believe in coincidences. He also doesn't believe in waiting for time to fill in the gaps for him. He'll do that himself. He decides to pay Father Caleb a visit.

If nothing else, he'll get the keys to his cottage a bit earlier than planned so he can get out of The Yew Tree and find some of that peace that he came here for.

****

The sun is a halo above the high branches of the trees by the time Pete walks down the hill to the church. Most of the early mist has been torn away by the breeze, and snatches of blue sky appear through scudding clouds. The birds are singing in the hedgerows and for the first time Pete starts to feel like this trip might have been a good idea after all.

A couple of kids run around the village green, chasing a ball, their screams of delight injecting bright colours into an otherwise grey atmosphere that envelops the village. A few adults huddle together, watching, and Pete feels the weight of their gaze as he crosses the road to the church. He raises a hand in a polite greeting that isn't returned. He's bemused to find himself chewing over that rejection as he walks up the path to the church door. The human soul can be frail, he thinks, even when time's been invested in building a suit of armour to house it.

He stops at the heavy wooden door. He can hear a choir within, a pleasing mixture of voices, and speculates that Penny might be amongst their number. He is wondering how to politely interrupt their practice when the door creaks open and Margaret squeezes through the narrow gap she's created.

'Mr Collins, isn't it?' she says. 'I thought I'd heard someone fumbling around out here.' She holds up a hand. 'Please, don't speak, you'll disturb the choir.' She pulls the door shut. 'There, that's better. Father Caleb has them where he wants them. Would be a terrible shame to interrupt the flow, wouldn't it? Can I help you at all?'

'I just wanted to speak with Caleb, I mean Father Caleb. I booked a cottage, Caprae Cottage, on the estate, and I'm told he's responsible for it. I was wondering if I could pick up the key a little early? I'm not due in until Monday, but well, I thought I'd check...'

'Oh! The pub's not to your liking then,' says Margaret with a sly smile. 'Poor Penny will be disappointed...'

'Oh no, it's not that, I just want some peace and quiet, and since I bumped into Father Caleb just this morning, you know, I thought it might be possible.'

'Well, it's not Father Caleb you need to speak to, you've been poorly informed. But it's your lucky day. I'm responsible for the upkeep of the Baddington Estate as well as the church. I have the keys to your cottage, but it's not ready yet, I'm afraid. Needs a good clean.'

'I'm OK with that, no need. I can give it a once-over, not averse to a bit of cleaning...'

'My, you are keen, aren't you. I suppose you want to get your money's worth, do you?' she says.

'I just thought I could get myself settled, it's no problem if that's not possible. I don't want to make life difficult for anyone.'

'Well, that's very generous of you, Mr Collins,' says Margaret, and Pete decides this woman really is a most disagreeable old bitch. The type of person who is always searching for seedlings of conflict. He takes a breath, wondering what it would be like to put a fist between her eyes. It's an unprofessional thought, and he pushes it to one side.

'Fine. Look, forget it. I'll wait until tomorrow.'

The door behind Margaret opens and Father Caleb joins them.

'Mr Collins. Peter! We meet again. What brings you to my door so soon!? Changed your mind about my sermon perhaps!'

'Mr Collins was enquiring about his cottage on the estate,' says Margaret. 'He thought he might be able to get in a day early.'

'Oh – is the pub not to your liking?' says Father Caleb with a concerned frown.

'No,' says Pete. 'The pub is just fine, I stocked up at the shop, like you said, and thought why not get myself settled, if it was free, but really it's no problem either way.'

'My dear Peter, of course we can accommodate you. It is in our interests for you to be comfortable and happy during your stay with us, is it not, Margaret? I am sure the cottage can be ready by this afternoon. It hasn't been occupied for a little while, has it? So if you don't mind a little dust...?'

'Perfect, but like I said, only if it's no trouble...'

'It's no trouble, is it, Margaret?' says Father Caleb.

Margaret's smile is more like a grimace. 'I'll get on with things,' she says. 'Leave it with me.'

'There we are!' says Father Caleb. His smile is positively beatific. 'Would you like a little tour of the church while you're here? The choir have finished up for now. I have time to spare, and nothing gives me more pleasure than showing it off!'

'Sure,' says Pete. Margaret dips into the church, returning a moment later with her coat. 'I'll be off then,' she says stiffly. They watch her walk down the path.

'She can be a funny old stick at times,' says Caleb, his voice low. 'But her heart's in the right place. She just lacks, well, let's just say, the subtlety required to win over the hearts as well as minds. Anyway, shall we?' says Caleb. He holds open the church door for Pete and ushers him inside.

The church seems even larger inside than it does from out, as if that were possible. The heavy doors lead to a stone-flagged chancel, flanked by chapels. The main body of the church stretches in front of them, neatly lined with dark wooden pews that suck light from the stained windows that arch the walls of the aisles on either side. The air hums in that peculiar way Pete associates with places of worship, like a tuning fork seeking a connection with tones that exist beyond the everyday. The choir gathers at the front of the church, speaking in low whispers that stop when they see Father Caleb with Pete.

'Impressive, isn't it?' says Caleb. 'There's been a church of some sort here since the Roman times. This one is an amalgamation of all the ones that followed, built one on top of each other over the centuries, so we get to keep a little bit of each. A reminder of the old days and ways. The original crypt is beneath our feet, if you can believe it? They don't make them like this anymore, do they?' he says with satisfaction.

Pete's always been sceptical of the Church. It took real money to build something like this, as indeed for any of the hundreds of churches that dig their foundations deep into the emotional substrate of this country. That money wasn't provided by the divine. There was no magic money tree, of course, no fountain that a benevolent God bequeathed to fund its places of worship. It was simply taken from the pockets of those that could afford it least, by light-fingered clerics who promised everything while having to deliver nothing. The ultimate Ponzi scheme, promising a salvation that was conveniently unknowable.

'They don't,' says Pete neutrally.

'We rebuilt part of the vestibule only a few years back, funded it all ourselves,' says Caleb, casting Pete a knowing look that makes him feel as if he might have just read his mind. 'It's the only way these days. You can't rely on those outside. No-one cares about an old church with a leaky roof in a place like Little Baddington. No-one except us, of course. So, we raised the money in the community. I confess a healthy contribution from Lord Baddington didn't hurt, there are only so many cake sales you can hold after all. But either way we got there. It is our achievement, and one we are all proud of.'

The choir has gathered up belongings and files dutifully past them. Father Caleb nods at them approvingly. Penny offers Pete a small nod of recognition, which is welcome amongst the otherwise blank, almost hostile stares he receives.

'Come. Let me show you something. As a sceptic you might find it amusing,' says Caleb. He leads Pete to the altar at the front of the church. 'This is the oldest part, dates to the eighth century. When all the lands around here formed part of the kingdom of Mercia.' He points Pete in the direction of a statue, carved into the stone wall. The edges of its shape have been worn by time, but its essential nature remains. It has the body of a man, and the head of a goat. 'Baphomet,' says Caleb. 'A pagan god, or demon if you prefer. Sitting here cheek by jowl in a Christian church, forming part of its very fabric. Remarkable! I approve of the juxtaposition! The very fact that the Almighty allows the presence of another within His church, within His place of worship, what does that tell us? That we can co-exist with difference if we are willing to try? In fact, that if we embrace that difference it might lead to wonderful things. Do you agree, Peter?'

'The sentiment's a good one, on the question of gods and demons I'm afraid I have no opinion,' says Pete.

'Hmm. Fair enough. You can leave the search for the divine to the likes of me. But we like our little friend Baphomet. He reminds us that although change is constant there is a place for the old ways in amongst the new. For that reason alone, he makes his welcome known in this church. As are you, Peter, should you change your mind during your stay with us.'

Pete offers a noncommittal smile that Father Caleb receives with a knowing one of his own.

'Anyway, those keys to the cottage. You will be itching to get over there, I'm sure. I mustn't keep you from your holiday. Margaret will be getting things in order for you, but I am sure there is a spare set of keys in the office, if you can wait a moment while I get them.'

'Of course, appreciate it,' says Pete.

Father Caleb makes his way to a small door on the far side of the pews. He ducks his head like a tortoise as he enters, leaving Pete in the silence of the church. The statue of the goat god is vaguely unsettling in a way Pete can't quite explain. He fails to see the pleasing juxtaposition that Father Caleb extols. Its presence hums in the silence of the church, a tuning fork to something unknowable. Pete finds himself scratching an itch that prickles under the skin on his arms, and is relieved when Father Caleb returns, tossing a set of keys between his hands.

'Are you OK, Peter?' he asks. A sly amusement shimmers beneath his concerned expression.

'Yes, just lost in thought for a moment.'

'Well, the Lord's house has a knack of triggering introspection. It is good to question oneself, Peter. Who you are, why you are. The big questions. Sometimes I find just sitting here, amongst all this history, it prompts me to dig a little deeper, you know. Not always a comfortable thing, but worthwhile, in the end. Here,' says Caleb. 'Take the keys to Caprae Cottage. I think you'll find it very comfortable, but of course if you need anything else, you know where to find me.'

Pete takes the keys from Father Caleb with a hand that isn't quite steady. 'Do you know what Caprae means, Peter?' he asks.

Pete shakes his head. He just wants to get outside and suck fresh air into his lungs that might dispel the sense of disconnect that's threatening to propel his breakfast over the floor.

'It means goat, in Latin! Isn't that a funny coincidence!'

****

Caprae Cottage is hidden at the end of an unmade track deep within the walls of the Baddington Estate. It sits amongst trees, small, squat, and less attractive than it looked on the website. Its tiled roof is covered in a carpet of thick moss and its metal window frames are freckled with rust. A spiral of smoke weaves its way into the trees from a chimney pot, fashioning a low fog that lends the shrouded clearing the aspect of a dark fairy-tale.

Pete navigates his hire car along a rutted mud track that he joined about 200 metres back, at the direction of a small wooden plaque in the hedgerow with the words 'Caprae Cottage' and an arrow burned into it. He notices there is a grey Suzuki 4x4 parked on a grass verge just beyond the cottage, and he wonders who it belongs to as he steers the car onto a hardstanding fashioned out of a patchwork of broken paving slabs. The front door of the cottage hangs open, like a dark mouth.

He leaves the engine running, opens his door and slides out. The air is heavy with the smell of woodsmoke. He hears rattling noises bouncing along the walls in the hallway and is immediately reassured that whoever's in there isn't exactly sneaking about. His internal temperature drops, and he calls out a cautious welcome.

'Hey, is there anyone in there?' he says.

The rattling stops and he hears busy footsteps. Margaret materialises from the gloom of the hallway.

'You're earlier than I expected,' she sniffs. She flicks on a light switch, bathing the hallway in a sickly yellow glow. 'You found it OK then? I often wonder if the signposts are clear enough. Sometimes we find you city folk wandering around in a daze as soon as you lose sight of tarmac.'

Pete grits his teeth and decides to play nice. If she wants a fight he's not going to rise to the bait. 'It was fine. Thanks for getting it ready for me. I see you've even lit a fire. That's very kind.'

Margaret's face flinches, as though being called kind is the last thing she wants. 'I'm about done. Just needed to air the place out and make sure the chimney's working. It's the crows, you see, always building nests in the pots. They can block it up and, well, we don't want to suffocate you now, do we?' The thought seems to cheer her up, and her face cracks into the same sly smile he witnessed back at the church.

'Just got to clear up the traps,' she says. 'You get a lot of little furry friends out here in the sticks, and they do love to find a nice dry place to stay. Not the company you'll be looking for, I suspect. So, if you can give me a moment, I'll just deal with that. Perhaps you can go collect your things, and then I'll show you how the boiler works. It's old and temperamental. A bit like me,' she says with a perfunctory smile.

Pete nods and head back to the car, popping the boot and retrieving his rucksack and his bags of shopping. A quick glance around confirms he will find the solace he's looking for. There is barely a sound beyond the faint caw of crows and the gentle rustle of leaves in the trees that surround them. He hoists his rucksack onto one shoulder and heads into the cottage.

The bulb in the hallway has warmed up, replacing the sickly glow with something more inviting. Off the hallway to his right is a small living room. Flames flickers lazily against the tarnished glass of a log burner. There is a sofa and a small table scattered with a few old books. A television hangs on the wall opposite. It looks cosy enough. Pete drops his rucksack on the floor and heads down the hallway to a small kitchen at the rear, passing another door that presumably hides a bedroom. He sets down his shopping on the worktop next to a Belfast sink. There is a window that looks out over a small lawn and paving area with the woods beyond.

'Pleasant view, isn't it?' says Margaret. She materialises behind him unannounced. 'It's very peaceful out here. There aren't that many cottages on the estate. His Lordship has always enjoyed his privacy, even now in his failing years. There are a few cottages for estate workers, but he insists the place isn't overrun with tourists. On that we agree.'

'Well, I'm lucky to be here then,' says Pete. He starts to unpack his shopping bags; in the hope it might encourage Margaret to leave him in peace. She shows no sign of taking the hint.

'The boiler's in the cupboard just there,' she says, pointing to the corner of the room. 'I've got it lit but you might want to give it a little while if you want a shower. The tank is small but still takes an hour or two to get hot. I'll just check the last of the traps and then I'll be out of your way.'

She disappears and Pete takes the opportunity to stow away his purchases. She returns as he puts the last of his things in the old fridge.

'All done,' she says brightly. She has a mouse in her hand. Its head pokes out of her fist, its nose twitching furiously. 'And we've captured a little interloper! Naughty thing. He must pay the price for his intrusion.' She smiles as she brings her thumb and forefinger together over the mouse's tiny head and squeezes. Pete hears the crack of tiny bones. Its head pops like a grape. 'That'll teach it,' she says softly.

Margaret observes the look on Pete's face. 'Oh, I'm sorry, Mr Collins, I didn't have you down as the squeamish type. Us country folk are used to dealing with vermin in a way that might seem a little... matter-of-fact to some. I hope I haven't upset you?'

Pete thinks upsetting him is pretty low on Margaret's list of concerns but is willing to play along with the charade a little longer if it'll get the crazy old bitch out of his cottage.

'You're fine, we deal with vermin in the city too,' says Pete.

'I'm sure you do, Mr Collins,' she says. 'I'll be off then. If you need anything you can call. There's a number next to the TV. The signal out here is a bit patchy at times, but if you drive up the end of the track and get back to the road it usually comes back in.'

Margaret reaches the door. 'You keep safe, Mr Collins!' she says. 'It'll get all kinds of dark out here when the sun goes down. Takes a bit of getting used to.'

The door closes and moments later he hears the chug of an engine and crunch of tyres on the track. The sound swells and fades, silence tumbling into its place.

****

Margaret is good to her word. Darkness falls quickly on the estate. It arrives seemingly without herald, wrapping itself sneakily around Caprae Cottage. The log burner is hungry, chewing its way through the small stack of cut wood that was left by the last occupant. Pete thinks he'll need to cut up some more tomorrow, and puts foraging for deadfall on his mental to-do list. The prospect of some simple physical activity is a pleasant one.

The cottage warms up nicely, the snug living room almost too hot, and Pete takes a moment to stand outside the front door. He looks up at the night sky, which is crisp and clear. He can't see any of the normal constellations, and after a minute or two of trying he gives up. The absence of those familiar celestial touchpoints makes him feel uncomfortable. Margaret has set his nerves running with her cryptic little barbs and penchant for mouse cruelty. What did Father Caleb say, she lacks the ability to capture hearts, or something like that? He thinks of the way her eyes shone when she popped the mouse's skull. *That is one crazy old bitch*...he thinks.

A pistol-shot crack of a branch breaking is followed by a sudden flurry of wings as crows roosting in the high trees are disturbed into flight. They caw with displeasure. Pete shuts the door and locks it behind him. He leaves the key in the lock, mindful that Margaret has a spare set. The thought of her popping up in the dead of the night as he sleeps isn't a happy one.

He returns to the living room, draws the curtains closed over the small window, and takes a seat by the log burner. He extracts his Glock from the hidden compartment at the bottom of his rucksack. He likes the feel of it in his hand, its presence reassuring, like an old friend. Without really thinking his hands restlessly release the magazine and break the gun down as if controlled by puppeteers' strings, the movement hypnotic and soothing. He listens to the pop and crack of burning wood and thinks about his past.

He was spat out of the care system when he hit sixteen, expelled with the same explosive force all of his fellow travellers in the land of foster care experienced when the state gleefully renounced its responsibilities. He remembers it being akin to being fired out of a cannon. You knew it was coming, but the loudness of the bang still surprised you.

He'd found himself homeless overnight and ended up following breadcrumbs back to his old haunts on the estates like a dutiful hound dog. It was there he, perhaps inevitably, fell into the company of old friends and acquaintances. The type of folk that his parents and teachers would've cautioned him against if they'd been around to do so. But they weren't, so he did what he had to do to survive and forged his own place in a uniquely precarious community. A world full of hyenas and lions. His path thereafter was well trodden, but his personal attributes allowed his own evolution to mutate at some point, a cross-species leap from hyena to lion, leading him to the place he now found himself, a hired gun of some repute, albeit with instructions to lay low.

Pete finds the burner phone Dave gave him back in the pub, what already feels a million years ago. It's boxy and looks as if it has been parachuted in from the early 2000s, but is perfect for its simple job, to connect him to Dave safely, securely and in a way that is completely untraceable.

He decides he should let Dave know he's arrived. He's also curious as to what the lay of the land is. The prospect of staying here for six weeks has become a rollercoaster. At the moment he is riding the crest of a wave that says getting the hell out would make sense.

IS THERE STILL HEAT? he texts.

He's kept an eye on the news since he finished the job, but the dizzying appetite for fresh headlines means even the ritual murder of a High Court judge doesn't carry enough weight to hold its place at the top of a feed for long, not these days. There seems to be nothing new to report. Which he decides is good news.

His phone vibrates.

WARM, BUT GETTING COOLER... it says. A moment passes. YOU OK...?

He's faintly surprised to get a follow-up question from Dave, who's not known for taking an interest beyond the essentials of professional discourse.

YES.... he replies, followed by....WHERE DID YOU FIND THIS PLACE? ITS FUCKING STRANGE.

He's not sure why he shared that sentiment with Dave and instantly wonders if he's overstepped some invisible line. His phone vibrates again.

SIT TIGHT... it says.

He waits a moment, his face illuminated by the glow of the phone screen. Pete doesn't like 'Sit tight'. It feels like an order, and he's not programmed to respond to those; instructions yes, orders, no. The phone is silent. His connection to Dave and his old life has been terminated for now. He tosses it onto the table where it slowly spins to a stop.

He decides he'll sleep with the Glock under his pillow.

****

Pete enjoys a surprisingly restful night's sleep, which he begrudgingly puts down to the company he keeps in the shape of his Glock. He's woken by the incessant cawing of crows and the tip-tap of avian footsteps as they pace back and forth across the roof of the cottage.

He snatches his burner phone from the bedside table. Dave hasn't sent any further messages. He folds his hands behind his head and slumps back onto his pillow, staring at patterns in the ceiling, following them down into his memories. Although not prone to introspection, he figures he's entitled to unpick some of his past, if it helps inform his future. His irritation with Dave hasn't been softened by a good night's sleep, and he thinks about how their paths first became entwined, wondering if a means of disentanglement may lie amongst the gossamer threads of experience that bind them.

Pete killed his first person aged just nineteen. A big bang moment that germinated a criminal infrastructure, building highways and byways that carried him from then to now. He'd been back on the estate for nearly three years when it happened. London was in flux, the city booming and fuelling an appetite for drugs that had flooded the streets. The opportunity coagulated into incendiary pools, the necessary ignition provided by a fevered scramble for money and power amongst those that sought to carve up and dominate this new market.

Pete was an established, if street-level, part of the machinery. His willingness to end life catapulted him up the food chain. He remembers doing it. Placing a gun to a head and pulling a trigger when no-one else would. He remembers how easy it was and not understanding why it changed the way people looked at him, and swiftly afterwards, the way they treated him.

He found himself extracted from the streets, redeployed, suddenly too useful to be left amongst the dirt and danger. He made friends in higher places. He was introduced to Dave. His real name and identity were erased. He became Pete.

He grabs his own phone, which is a good degree 'smarter' than the one Dave provided. The Wi-Fi is as unsteady as a toddler, and his VPN is intermittent, but he pulls up a map of the area and starts to build a better picture of where he is, the access roads around him, before his mind inevitably turns towards evaluating the way unfriendlies might be able to triangulate him. The paranoia that drives his thought process is as natural as breathing, and he embraces it readily and without embarrassment.

He sees the road that brought him into Little Baddington continues, crossing a river and heading north towards Leamington Spa. There is a pop-up on Google that suggests a problem with a bridge, but it's dated 2019 and so he figures it must be a glitch. He doesn't have any reason to go to the village today especially when doing so risks being pressganged into church for Sunday service, so he resolves to take a drive out in the opposite direction later, after he's had breakfast.

****

Pete pours boiling water into a mug and tosses in a teabag. He looks out the kitchen window across the lawn as it brews. He can see an old outhouse at the end of the garden. Its door hangs on one hinge drunkenly, and the roof is encased in ivy. The mist is slowly returning, its light fingers snatching at the corners of the grass, tucking them away into deep pockets. The garden furniture, painted white, seems to glow in the ambient light.

The cottage doesn't feel like a holiday let. It doesn't have the resonance of occupation, not even transitory occupation. It just feels like an empty house. The Belfast sink is unblemished. The taps are unsullied by watermarks. The worktops are wooden but show little signs of wear and tear that would come from the careless use you expect from holiday guests. He opens a kitchen drawer. It is stocked with a variety of implements. He notices a few of them still carry a shop label. The toaster spits his bread out noisily. He chances a peek inside. The guts of the toaster are crumb free. He's not convinced Margaret was that thorough in her hasty spring clean.

Pete has a sudden sense of standing on a stage set, one that has been carefully prepared to receive its latest performer. He fishes the teabag out of his mug and takes a sip, disquiet uncoiling in his stomach like a languid snake.

Chapter 9

The roads within the Baddington Estate are poorly maintained. Potholes pepper the tarmac, offering a cratered no man's land that Pete tentatively negotiates in his Audi. He has visions of shredded tyres and broken axles, and all the associated paperwork and ball ache that'd accompany that misfortune.

The grass verges are overgrown and stuffed with the remnants of summer's decaying ant nests. Picket fences that once shone white are dull with decay. Baddington Hall looms up ahead. Pete's decided to give it a quick drive-by on his way out of the estate. It transmits faded grandeur in keeping with its surroundings. He can't imagine anyone living within its crumbling walls. The Georgian pillars that support the upper floors look like a power lifter who's bitten off more than he can chew. The roof slumps like a camel's back. Pete pulls his car over onto a gravel driveway and gets out. Wrought iron gates prevent any further progress. The gates are housed within stone pillars, topped by a replica of the statue Father Caleb showed him back in the church. A goat god astride a twisted tree.

Pete spots movement. A figure is being wheeled out of the broad entrance to the house. Even allowing for the distance, he can see a tall skeletal man, sitting bolt upright in a wheelchair, his legs covered with a heavy blanket. He's accompanied by a woman who fusses over him before returning inside. The old man doesn't move as he waits, seemingly frozen, gazing over a crumbling dominion, a Caesar whose Rome has already burned.

It must be Lord Baddington, thinks Pete, the benevolent patron of Father Caleb's community, fixing church roofs while neglecting his own it would seem. The breeze picks up, ruffling the blankets around his legs. One flips off and dances across the steps that lead down to the gravel drive. He doesn't seem to notice its departure. The wind lifts straggly grey hair off a face that is hollow and lifeless. After a moment his nurse returns. She hustles down the steps and retrieves the blanket. It is secured around his legs before she wheels him back into the house. Pete thinks Father Caleb might need to invest a bit of time in his patron, as on first impression he doesn't look like a reliable source of long-term funding.

He returns to his car, starts the engine and leaves Baddington Hall in his rear-view mirror.

****

On the outskirts of the village, a battered green Land Rover idles by the roadside. Its engine is running, its exhaust a gently shuddering pipe, puffing fumes up into the morning sky. The windows are steamed up, even though the fans inside are running at full tilt. Brothers Noah and Joseph Burgh sit together in the cab. They are under instruction to watch the road. If they see a blue Audi heading north, they are to follow it, discreetly.

Joseph is overexcited. Noah's familiar with the signs. They are twins, like two peas in a pod, as his dear mother used to say, but much of that similarity ends with how they look. Noah is smart. He's a thinker, not prone to rash decisions. Joseph is the opposite. He's always lived on instinct, making him impulsive and reckless. Educationally subnormal had been the assessment by his teachers, all those years ago, long before anyone really cared about such things. Noah had been no less a troubling character; in fact, he'd been more so. When he did something nasty, he'd thought about it. Malice aforethought was a given. Joseph, on the other hand, simply reacted. Although the outcome was often the same, in terms of damage done, it was intentional cruelty that gave Noah's his distinguishing characteristic. Unsurprisingly the pair of them had been ejected from one school after another, always as a pair, as if their umbilical cord had never been cut, instead pumping perpetual mischief between them. It'd been inevitable they would bid farewell to the school system as soon as the authorities could reasonably look the other way. Life since had been colourful, to put it mildly.

They are following Margaret's orders, and when she gives an order, Noah knows you take it seriously. You listen and follow instructions precisely. You don't get carried away, and unfortunately that's what Joseph always does. Noah doesn't want to upset Margaret. No-one in the village does.

'How much longer?' says Joseph sullenly. He's eying the end of the lane that adjoins the main road. It's the only way off the estate, and so if their target is going to materialise, it's from here that he'll have to depart.

'Joe, I don't know. We've just been asked to watch is all. Nothing more. Settle down, you're wearing me out.'

Joseph purses his lips and blasts out an exasperated sigh. He flicks the glove box open and closed a few times before Noah stops him with a strained smile. 'Just sit still, Joe,' he says with patience he doesn't feel.

They share a house in the village. It isn't huge, and isn't nearly big enough for Noah, given his brother's questionable hygiene and numerous other unsavoury habits, but it's a home and he is well aware, in the real world, it would be far beyond the means of the two of them to rent it, let alone own it as they now do. But then that's the secret sauce of Little Baddington. The trade-off was you had to do as you were told from time to time, to play your part in protecting the common good. Experience taught him this was a broad remit, one that required a stiff back and a strong stomach. That's fine with Noah. He knows which side his bread is buttered, and besides, he took it upon himself to look after Joseph. Although well advanced in years, he is essentially still a child. One that is safe in the village, where he's understood and tolerated. Anywhere else, well, he'd find himself locked up within a week, such is his endless capacity for ill-considered mischief.

'This is boring. I thought we'd be tracking this fella, not sat here like idiots all morning,' says Joseph.

'Have you got somewhere else you need to be?' says Noah through gritted teeth.

Joseph grunts and settles into morose silence, arms folded across his chest. Noah reminds himself that, despite appearances, he is dealing with a fifty-six-year-old man, not a surly teenager. Blood truly is thicker than water, he thinks.

'Look, Joe, we're doing this for Margaret. It's not a lot to ask, and besides we don't have much to do on the estate. The birds are out, and other than us boys, there's no guns this year, you know that. We'll have some sport later when we've finished up with this. That'll make up for it,' says Noah.

He can see Joseph thinking it over. The cogs turn slowly, but they do at least turn. Noah knows the prospect of shooting a few birds will liven him up, as it will him. It's what they know best, having worked the estate for a lifetime, from back when they used to get huge shooting parties to blast away at countless pheasants. Tips had been good in those days. He misses them, but it's the way of things, or so says Margaret anyway. His Lordship is to be protected, she says, from those who would do him harm. Noah knows that Margaret really means those who would do harm to the estate. His Lordship's kids and their greedy fingers, keen to split up the pie and consign the old ways of Little Baddington to history.

A blue Audi appears at the junction. It indicates right and drives past them. Noah doesn't think the driver gave them so much as a look.

''Ere we go,' says Noah.

He puts the Land Rover in gear, gooses the accelerator and follows.

****

Pete notices the Land Rover as soon as he pulls up to the junction and flicks his indicator to the right. He thinks there were two men in the cab, albeit the window is steamed up and he didn't want to make a big show of looking as he drove past.

It's amateur hour stuff, thinks Pete, as he observes whoever is driving the Land Rover make a show of hanging back fifty yards, presumably in some attempt to look 'casual'. Tailing someone discreetly in the middle of nowhere, when you are the only two cars on the road for miles, is an exercise in futility. Pete takes what inference he can from the fact the occupants of the vehicle are even trying and concludes that amateur hour is, for him at least, good news.

The road weaves through fields and woodland, submerging in and out of shade. The satnav indicates he will shortly reach the border of Little Baddington, where the road passes over a river. He navigates a tight corner and hits the brakes. There's a tattered 'police aware' sign strung across the road like forgotten bunting. A series of battered cones are scattered across the tarmac. One sits upside down in the verge. Grass grows over it.

The road beyond rises, following the curvature of the bridge, but then disappears, leaving a lip to pout over water flowing below. Pete exits his car. He hears the Land Rover approaching behind him but chooses to ignore it. He wanders up the road, passing under the police line, and peers over the edge. The detritus of the broken bridge fills the river below, creating a rapid that bubbles and roars. The road on the other side offers an unbroken promise of travel away from Little Baddington.

Pete hears doors slamming. He turns, sees two men and experiences a moment of distortion when he recognises both of them from The Yew Tree. They are twins, and as near identical as he has ever seen.

'Morning,' says Pete, raising a hand in greeting.

The man nearest nods a welcome. The one behind him simply stares.

'Morning to you,' says Noah. He has an accent like treacle and looks as though he enjoys the taste of it in his throat as he shapes his words. 'You've come across our little problem then. No road north out of Little Baddington these days, I'm afraid. It's one way in, one way out.'

'So I see,' says Pete.

'Don't fret, nothing worth seeing up that way anyway, is there, Joe?' says Noah.

'Nowt,' says Joseph.

'You staying on the estate, sir?' says Noah.

'I am,' says Pete, thinking that stating the obvious must be a pastime around these parts.

'Well you might as well get yourself back there. This road been out for a long time and no-one seems in much of a rush to fix it. We don't mind so much, stops the through traffic you know, keeps the village nice and quiet, but if you want to go sightseeing you'll have to head back to Moreton, and go the long way around. Can't say I'd bother, if I were you. Plenty to keep you occupied in Little Baddington if you knows where to look.'

'Right,' says Pete. They stand in front of him as if waiting for something more. The silence they bring has edges.

'You from London then?' says Joseph. 'That's what we heard, didn't we, Noah? You were at the pub the other night. Noah says you didn't stop for long? Can't say I blame you, Craig fella's a pillock!'

They break into mean-spirited laughter. Pete says nothing and as their laughter tapers off, he feels a divide go up between them, as if he has picked a side, and it's the wrong one.

'Guess you London types stick together,' growls Joseph.

'Not really. I just keep myself to myself, you know,' says Pete. 'Don't make a habit of getting involved in other people's business. I came down here for that peace and quiet you mentioned. That's all.'

'Ignore Joe, Mr Collins,' says Noah. 'He's a bit hot-headed and has a countryman's distrust of those from far away. He doesn't mean anything by it.'

Pete raises an eyebrow metaphorically. 'I don't remember giving you my name?' he says mildly.

Noah smiles, revealing yellowing teeth. 'It's a small place…..news travels fast. We don't get much excitement around here, so a new face, well, it's worthy of a bit of gossip. Don't let it trouble you,' he says.

'I won't,' says Pete. 'It's been nice meeting you gents, but if that's everything, I'll hop back in my car and decide what to do with the day.'

'Of course, sir, you mind how you go,' says Noah. He steps to one side, dipping his head in a sarcastic bow, and allows Pete to pass. They stand in the road watching, as he reverses his car and heads back towards the village.

Chapter 10

Joseph sips his pint. He sits at the bar in The Yew Tree. He's on his usual stool, the one nearest the door. He drinks alone. Craig served him, disappearing back into the other bar as quickly as he could. He didn't even try to make small talk, like he does when Noah's with him. A bubble of acid rises up from his stomach and scorches his throat.

Noah has business with Father Caleb. Community meetings, he calls them. It irks Joseph that he's never invited to those meetings. He knows people think he's too stupid to be involved, and suspects they might even be right, but feels they could invite him all the same. After all, he's been around as long as his brother, he knows all the secrets and lies that bind them together, and it wouldn't hurt to show him a little respect every now and again. He grimaces, his thoughts as bitter as the liquid he swallows from his pint glass.

Without a handbrake, Joseph is already well past his usual midweek limit. Not that he thinks he needs a limit, but Noah says he does. If he drinks too much his head grows thick with ugly thoughts. Thinking isn't good for him. He stores up grievances the way a squirrel collects nuts, burying them within dusty corners of his subconscious, a hoard of animosity that dates back many years. Sometimes he hears mocking laughter bubbling up from beneath the soil.

The fella from London, Collins, is a fresh deposit and his restless anger uncovers it, tossing it between mental fingers. They're all the same, the folks from outside. They swan around, acting like they own places, like all the people that belong there are stupid and worthless. Collins had looked at Joseph like he was stupid, just like they all did.

Noah says Little Baddington is special, that it still belongs to them that are local, that they've fixed it, so no-one can come and steal what is theirs, but Joseph feels a throbbing anger anyway, the type of anger that's underpinned much of his adult life. That anger usually only goes away if he replaces it with pain. Not his own, someone else's.

The door to the local bar opens and he's joined by Ezekiel, or Zeke as they call him. He works with him and Noah on the estate, as do most of the local men. Lord Baddington and his deep pockets remain the singular teat from which they suck enthusiastically.

''Evenin', Joe,' says Zeke, clapping a hand onto his shoulder. 'How's you?'

Joseph smiles. It's the type of smile that'd make anyone take a careful step back, the non-verbal equivalent of a landmine.

'Better for seeing you,' he slurs. 'Grab yourself a pint, I've got a favour to ask you.'

****

Pete's spent a productive afternoon at the cottage. There is now fresh wood in the log pile, neatly stacked, and his shoulders and back hum with the righteous warmth of physical activity. Night has drawn its cloak around the cottage, and he sits in the living room, the wood burner pumping out a fierce crackling heat that is making his eyeballs squeak, while he taps away on his laptop.

He pulls up his browser history and clicks on the link for Little Baddington Estate, the one Dave sent him so he could load directions into his satnav. The laptop has a think, the search icon whirling, before displaying a 'website cannot be found' message. He clicks again and gets the same result. He gets up and checks the Wi-Fi router. It's been temperamental since his arrival, but the glowing lights on the front of the box indicate a signal is being received and pumped around the cottage. His laptop agrees, as a few alternative searches, 'Little Baddington estate lettings', 'Little Baddington cottages for rent', throw up random search results, but the website he's seen, the one with the picture of the grand old house on it, and the booking instructions for Caprae Cottage, no longer exists.

Pete frowns. Paranoia, whilst his trusted companion, requires checks and balances. A degree of interrogation is merited here, thinks Pete, so it doesn't radically distort his decision making. The case of a vanishing website could mean something or nothing. At this stage he is willing to settle for somewhere in between, and certainly isn't inclined to go overboard.

He settles back into the soft embrace of the sofa, pondering his next move. In the distance he hears the faint growl of an engine. The sound swells, accompanied by sweeping light across the curtains that cover a living-room window that faces the front of the property. He hears the crackle of tyres on wet mud. The light vanishes along with the sound of the engine. Doors open and shut loudly. Whoever's visiting him isn't being discreet, which he decides is a good thing. What follows is rather less good. Something hits the cottage with a thump. A moment later the window implodes, and a piece of rock bounces off the log burner with a metallic clang and makes itself acquainted with the fireside rug.

Pete is on his feet instantly. He moves fast, opening the front door, triggering the security light that sits just above the porch. The area in front of the house is bathed in sudden light. Frozen within it, Pete sees one of the brothers from earlier that day, either Joe or Noah, he can't tell which. He stands besides Pete's car, with one hand on its roof as if to steady himself. He continues to weave slightly, as if blown by a hidden breeze. He is accompanied by a younger man. He is short, but thickset with a crop of reddish hair that springs up from the side of his head as if he's received an electric shock. He's standing to the right of Joe/Noah. Neither of them seems to be armed. Pete can see a Land Rover parked at the foot of the drive. The passenger door is ajar and a weak bulb glows within the cabin, which otherwise seems to be empty.

'London!' shouts Joe/Noah. ''Ere 'e is, Mr Big Shot London.' His words are thick and slurred. Pete can smell him now, a heady stink of booze that rides the fresh night air. His companion laughs. Pete dials down his internal temperature slightly. A couple of drunks isn't much of an issue. They can do what they want to the cottage, it isn't his, and the stupid fuckers would end up paying for any damage.

'Disturb ya, did we... Looooondon!' says Joe/Noah. He totters away from the car, his ability to stay upright tested with every step.

'Looks like you boys might have had a drink or two?' says Pete. 'Perhaps you've got mixed up and come to the wrong place.'

'Naaah, London, we're in the right place, ain't we, Zeke, know what we're doing...'

'Sure are,' says Zeke. He gives Pete a smile that drips overconfidence. He tosses a rock up and down in one hand.

'You do know this isn't my house, right? You can smash the fucking thing to the ground for all I care, but I'd prefer you didn't do it while I was inside,' says Pete.

'Ooooh, prefer we didn't do it,' says Joe/Noah. They bark caustic laughter. Pete can feel a barometer rise a notch. There's pressure here, he thinks, something that's going to be released, one way or another.

'Maybe we wants to do it, bit of sport an' all that,' says Joe/Noah. 'Do y' like sports, London?'

They edge closer. The air grows thick with storm clouds, ones pregnant with violence. Pete evaluates the threat. Like any sensible person, he prefers to avoid close-quarter combat. There are too many variables, and his ability to control them is limited, at least when compared with the luxury of taking a well-planned shot from a distance, but if he must, he will. The twitching, adrenaline-fuelled movements of these two is making it feel like a racing certainty. They fancy themselves with the misinformed arrogance of true locals. They are the hard men around here, no doubt holding court in that Local Bar, telling tales, making sure anyone unfortunate enough to wander into their kingdom uninvited is under no illusion as to who rules the roost. Pete suspects they've cracked many heads over the years, of those that didn't belong, or were too slow to realise. But that insularity is a weakness. They look at Pete and see what they want to see. They see a man from away, a thin man, from a weak city, who is out of place and out of his depth.

'I don't want any trouble, lads,' says Pete, in a last-ditch effort to manage the situation without fists. 'Just take yourselves off home and we can forget about it.'

Joe/Noah rushes at him, but his movements are slow and telegraphed. Pete steps to one side and rolls him over his knee. He lands in a bush where he wallows momentarily like a turtle flipped on its back. Zeke is evidently less drunk, and he comes in swinging. His attacks are vicious but linear. Pete ducks the first two blows, glancing a third off his shoulder. He brings his forehead down onto Zeke's nose. There is a satisfying crunch that accompanies an explosion of blood. Zeke falls back, gasping.

Joe/Noah extracts himself from the shrubbery and gets unsteadily to his feet. He bares his teeth and growls like a dog. They make wary circles on the lawn as Zeke splutters blood from his nose.

'Come on then, you fucker,' snarls Joe/Noah. He moves surprisingly fast, coming in low and grappling at Pete's waist. He's strong and Pete's pushed backwards. A fist slams into his side. Pete decides a few more of them would get uncomfortable and it's time to bring this little skirmish to a halt. A short sharp shock is required, before Zeke gets his wind back. Pete has a little trick, one he learned years ago, one that delivers showstopper levels of pain. He digs his thumbnail into the top of Joe/Noah's ear and wrenches the cartilage down with all the force he can muster.

Joe/Noah shrieks and lets go of Pete. His hand races to the side of his face, finding a ragged hole where his ear once was. Blood fountains over his hand and he howls up at the night sky. 'My fucking ear, you bastard!! Arrghhh, you fucking...my ear....' he screams.

'Zeke,' says Pete. 'Get your arse over here and help your friend...'

Zeke looks at Pete with wide eyes, shock writ large over his features, rendering him compliant. 'Joe,' he says, his voice muffled and nasal, 'You alright, Joe?'

'He's torn my fucking ear off!!'

Pete watches Joe carefully. He thinks it'll be considerably easier to tell the brothers apart next time he sees them, and a small smile ghosts across his face.

'I'll fucking get you for this. My brother...you wait,' says Joe. His voice is high and whiny but the fight seems to have gone out of this particular dog, and Joe allows Zeke to put a hand on his shoulder and lead him away.

'I'm sure you will,' says Pete. 'But have a little think before you come back, I won't be as accommodating next time.' He tosses Joe's severed ear at them. It hits Zeke on the sleeve and plops into the grass. Joe sweeps it up and cups it in his hands as they stagger back to the Land Rover, squabbling as they climb into the cab.

Pete briefly wonders if they might have a weapon in the vehicle, given that most country folk seem welded to shotguns, but the engine fires up and they wheelspin away. The night settles around him and he gratefully allows silence to fill his ears.

He listens to his heartrate slow and wonders what the hell Dave was thinking sending him to this little corner of Hell.

Chapter 11

Doctor Elijah Brown's practising certificate was withdrawn many years ago, sometime before his sixty-sixth birthday. His hands hadn't been particularly steady back then, and the additional years on the clock have done little to improve matters. Joseph Burgh is painfully aware of these facts. His face was ghostly pale when he was escorted to the Doc's house and seems to have found new depths since, to the point where he looks faintly transparent under the glare of the lights in the Doc's kitchen, which currently doubles as an emergency room.

The Doc's hand wavers as he threads a second suturing needle. Joseph's tattered ear has been successfully reattached, and the Doc is pleased with his work. The secondary sutures will pull Joe's skin tightly over the cartilage, and he's confident that in the fullness of time, when the wounds heal, and provided they avoid infection, Joe will have a full set of ears again, and be none the worse for his ordeal. He swabs iodine over the site, and the purple liquid runs down Joe's neck and combines with bloodstains on his shirt collar.

The Doc's audience looks less confident. Father Caleb and Margaret watch him from the other side of his kitchen. Their nervous expressions indicate the assurances they gave Joe, when they convinced him to go to the Doc and not to the hospital in Moreton, were not quite as well founded as they'd suggested.

Noah stands at the Doc's shoulder, breathing like a horse at a stable gate, as he watches the needle slide in and out of his brother's flesh. He is effervescent with rage. It boils under the skin of his head, rattling his skull and making it difficult to focus. His eyes pulse in time with his chainsaw heart. Revenge is all he can think about. He would've been at Pete Collins' door already had he not been in the company of Father Caleb and Margaret when Zeke brought a bloodied Joe to the doors of the church. Their meeting finished, Maria and Herschel had already headed off into the night, and he too was about to leave when Joe had burst in. It had taken all of Father Caleb's powers of persuasion to stop him grabbing his shotgun and administering some local justice. Pete Collins did not belong to him. That's what Margaret said. And what Margaret says is law. He grimaces, the thought bitter enough to make his stomach clench like a fist.

He gives Joe's shoulder a squeeze of solidarity. When they were kids they shared wounds, the pain and discomfort, the connection between them as powerful as it was unknowable. He's sure he can feel his ear twinge with each stitch.

'Nearly there, young Joseph. You've been very brave,' says the Doc, his patter familiar and as old as he is. Everyone in the village has been looked after by Doctor Brown at some point or another. He's part of the tapestry of their lives, woven between them all. 'You'll be fine. We'll need to keep an eye on it, make sure the stitches take, and keep that wound clean, no messing around. An infection will put paid to all my hard work, and I'm quite pleased with what I've done here tonight. I'll get a bandage on that, and you'll have to change it regular. Noah can help you.'

Joseph grunts in reply. The embarrassment of being roughed up by that pansy from London eats away at him. Zeke has only sketched out what happened, broad details, nothing more. The truth was far more painful than the shaky stitches applied to his ear.

'You show me what to do, Doc, and I'll do it,' says Noah.

'We'll all support Joseph,' says Father Caleb. 'It is a savage thing that's been done to him. It won't go unpunished. I can assure you of that.' He looks meaningfully at Noah. Margaret gives him a nod of assent, and Noah takes his cue from that.

'What now then?' says Noah.

'You get home, get some rest. And in the morning, you, Zeke and a couple of your boys are going to go up to Caprae and collect Mr Collins for me,' says Margaret. 'And then we'll get you the justice you crave, but my way, don't mess it up. Bring him to the church.'

****

Pete sleeps lightly. His Glock plays mistress, keeping him company.

Before he bedded down, he messaged Dave, using the burner phone. He received no reply. The phone is still mute in the morning. Because the tech is so basic, he can't even tell if Dave's seen his message.

The morning brings introspection. Pete surveys the scene of the crime. The curtains in the living room flutter in the breeze like an apology. He's cleaned up most of the broken glass but thinks a few shards might be hiding in the rug, waiting to get a taste of unsuspecting feet.

He decides he wants out of Little Baddington. This place nags at him, like a piece of meat caught between his teeth, his unease an insistent tongue prodding away, unwilling to let it go. Dave, and his order to sit tight, can fuck off. Dave's going to have to answer to Pete when he gets back to London.

He dresses quickly. It's in his nature to search the clear blue sky for thunderclouds. It's an approach that's served him well and he's not inclined to change now. He supposes it's a legacy of his years in care when he could only rely on himself. Until recently he's thought about those days seldom. They are not warm thoughts, instead an echoey reminder of cold hallways, of time in corners, facing a wall that smelled of damp and rot. Pete shakes his head. *Best left buried*, he thinks, *those corpses are restless.*

He checks the Glock, the habit allowing him to toss a final shovel of dirt on his memories and focus on the now. He cleans the barrel and double-checks the clip. It's fully loaded. Beneath the false bottom of his rucksack are two more clips, giving him a total of eighteen rounds. He puts the two spares in his jacket pocket. It's not as many as he'd like, but he's travelled light. This was, after all, meant to be pleasure, not business.

He has his cutlery as a back-up. One is a fixed blade. One is a karambit. He prefers the fixed blade if things get up close and personal. He can draw it faster, with minimum risk of snagging. He's seen a few cases of switchblade failure and knows the first few seconds of any hand-to-hand duel are vital. Hesitation is what kills you, and Pete doesn't hesitate. In the end he settles for the karambit. It's a nasty little knife, its smaller curved blade is like a vendetta and is in keeping with the mood.

Pete tucks the Glock into his belt and fastens the karambit to his inner thigh. He heads to the kitchen, fills a kettle and puts a teabag in a mug. He's not in a rush now and wants to take a moment to think. This has become a job, which means he needs to approach it professionally. He needs to look for thunderclouds in the sky.

He starts remediation. He will erase his presence in this cottage as thoroughly as he can. He selects some disinfectant spray from a cupboard under the kitchen sink and puts on a pair of bright yellow rubber gloves that he finds. He thinks about where he has been in the short time he's been in the cottage, and starts work in the bathroom, carefully wiping all the surfaces he may have touched. He works his way through the cottage methodically, not rushing. The relative brevity of his stay works in his favour and after forty minutes or so of careful cleaning, he is satisfied that most traces of him are gone. As a final measure he locates a vacuum, runs it over the carpets and sofas, and then bags up the dust and hair he's collected. He also strips the bed and places the sheets and pillowcase in the same bin bag, along with the rubber gloves. The bag will be burned later once he's put a comfortable number of miles between himself and Little Baddington.

He sweeps up the keys to his Audi, hoists his rucksack onto one shoulder and opens the front door. It's 8.30 am and time to go.

Pete pauses, taking in a mist-shrouded tree line and the soft caw of crows high up in the branches. He feels watched but puts his jitters in a box and heads to his car, releasing the boot and tossing his rucksack into it.

There is something spread across the windscreen. A dead animal of some kind, purplish pink in colour, steaming softly in the cold morning air. Its torso has been butterflied open, its four limbs pinned to the corners of the windscreen. The head is flattened, but Pete can make out nubs on the top of its broken skull. He thinks it's a lamb or something like that, and one that probably never had the opportunity to draw a breath, looking every inch like it was ripped from its mother's womb before being filleted and deposited on his car. The knife marks on its torso are precise and clean. The work of someone who knows their way around a carcass, a butcher, or maybe a gamekeeper, he thinks. The eyes have been removed, either by whoever did this, or possibly an opportunist crow.

Pete looks around for something to help him remove the carcass from the windscreen. Although he doesn't consider himself particularly squeamish, its embryonic provenance makes his stomach churn. He catches a glimpse of movement on the lane, beyond the hedgerow that provides a border to the cottage.

'Hey!' he shouts. 'Hey, you!'

A pale face, partially shrouded by a hood, flashes in his direction, before sprinting away. Pete follows, slipping momentarily in thick mud. He sees someone dive through a gap in a hedgerow, about twenty metres up the lane, where the mist is thick and soupy. Pete knows he's going to lose sight of his target quickly if he doesn't get moving.

He hustles up the lane, following footprints through the hedgerow, into a small field which mercifully, is fallow and unploughed. If the mud had been thick Pete would have no chance catching up with his fleet-footed prey, who has already made it to the far side. Pete hears the muffled clang of a kissing gate.

He picks up his pace, his heart rate rising appreciably. He wrenches open the gate, dives through and finds himself at the edge of a large ploughed field. Here, the mist has receded, torn into threads by a morning breeze that plays across the field. His prey has already made it to the far side. Quite how he has managed to move so fast Pete doesn't know, but if he hits the tree line, he's lost him. His hand has retrieved the Glock from his waistband without really thinking, and he finds himself following the fleeing figure down the Glock's spine in his outstretched hand. There is another brief flash of a pale face as his prey looks back at him and then he is gone, into the trees.

Pete lowers the Glock, exasperated and a little embarrassed that he drew his weapon. A handgun, even one as powerful as a Glock, is wholly unsuited to the distance anyway. He takes a furtive look around himself and is relieved to see he's alone. In doing so he is swamped with a feeling of déjà vu. He is in the field where he spooked himself on his morning run.

To his right is the first of a series of figures standing upright in the field. Without the disorientating mist, it's now clear what they are. Scarecrows. The one closest to him is failing to fulfil its essential purpose, as two fat black birds perch on one of its outstretched arms. They watch Pete approach but show no sign of flying away.

The pumpkin head has deteriorated. Its blistered skin weeps brown tears and is slumped to one side. He catches a whiff of sweet carrion on the breeze, its source confirmed as one of the birds digs its thick beak into a crescent eye slit and tugs out a fleshy blob, throwing its head back to rock it down its throat. Its efforts are rewarded by a croaky *caawww* of approval from its mate. Pete knows that smell all too well.

The body that is strung up within the tattered clothing of the scarecrow has been there for a while judging by the smell, which is sickly sweet, like cinnamon mixed with dog shit. Time's done a bit to diminish its potency, but it still catches in the back of Pete's throat. The ragged overcoat that covers its torso is riven with weeping stains. The corpse's hand is exposed, the skin thin and greyish green in colour, stretched over deadfall bones. Pete can make out a small tattoo on the papery skin, just above the wrist. The symbol is familiar. It's the mark of an assassin. An affectation that he's never considered good business, but the type of thing beloved by low-level amateurs and blowhards that circle within the criminal community. Whoever was hung out here to become crow food, was not from Little Baddington. It was someone who got themselves disappeared.

He counts three more scarecrows, in varying stages of decay, and wonders who else might be hidden inside them.

Another crow lands and starts to peck away at the scarecrow's pumpkin head. A few weedy looking maggots scatter like rice onto the soil beneath.

****

Pete retraces his steps to the cottage.

The dead animal on his car has cooled. He finds an old sack in the woodshed and uses that to pluck it off his windscreen. He tosses the body in the hedgerow. The bloody residue it leaves behind looks as if it's going to test the capacity of the windscreen wipers and so he heads back into the house and gets a bucket of water. He sloshes it over the windscreen, and the wipers swipe back and forth rapidly, creating a pink foam that runs down the side of the car, pooling on the gravel. A few bits of ragged flesh cling stubbornly to the blades. Pete takes a look at the woods, feeling the oppressive weight of an unseen gaze. He can imagine a few of the local goons having a good laugh at his expense.

The only way he can get out by car is via the village, his other route extinguished by the fallen bridge. He has vague thoughts of meeting a crowd of villagers with torches and pitchforks. He's nervous, and gallows humour isn't alleviating that. He has little choice but to head that way and hope for the best. Going across country isn't an option. Little Baddington is a long way from anywhere.

Annoyed at his own jitters, Pete decides to get moving. Inertia is an enemy. He starts his car, peering through a windscreen that now only carries a memory of its gory deposit. He drives down the narrow track that will lead him back to the main road, dropping the window so he can get some fresh air, hoping it will help clear his head, which feels muddy and slow. His Glock is on the passenger seat next to him. He doesn't remember putting it there, but it feels like good company.

The track is longer than he remembers, and Pete's wondering if he's manged to miss his turning when he spots the tarmac estate road through the hedgerow that runs to his right. The car takes a final lurching bump off the track and resets itself on a smooth surface that feels like safe returns. He gooses the accelerator, and the countryside starts to blur alongside him. He's driving too fast for unfamiliar roads, but at this moment is willing to chance it.

He rounds the next corner, and the Audi suddenly feels flabby. The back end drifts, and Pete finds himself wrestling with the steering wheel to regain control. Up ahead he spots a Land Rover. It's parked across the road. He slams on the brakes and the car fishtails, churning up the verge. The dense hedgerow provides a rapid percussive accompaniment on the passenger door as the car grinds to a halt.

Pete lets out a whistling breath and unpicks his white-knuckle grip from the steering wheel.

Through the windscreen he observes three men exit the Land Rover. The first is Noah, unless Joe's miraculously grown back his ear overnight. He has a shotgun draped over his arm. The next is Zeke, his nose a purply red and sporting dark bruises under his eyes. He stands alongside him. He also has a shotgun which is pointed in Pete's direction. The third man he doesn't recognise. He's big and has dirty straw-coloured hair that's tucked under a red cap with the letters C.A.S.E on it. He doesn't carry a gun. Instead, he has an axe, a big one, the kind that Pete imagines lumberjacks swing at trees. They all telegraph bristling hostility.

A quick glance to his left confirms his Glock is no longer on the passenger seat. His sudden halt has flung it into the foot well. Any move in that direction will likely ignite some excitement in the men pointing their guns at him, so Pete keeps his hands on the steering wheel, where they can see them.

'Mr Collins,' shouts Noah. 'You're in an awful rush this morning? Out of the car. Now. Nice and slow.'

Pete assesses his position. Zeke look sufficiently wired to start squeezing the trigger of his shotgun. The axe looks well acquainted with the big fella's hands. The existence of dilemma provokes a familiar response from his nerve endings, injecting him with an unlikely calm. Pete breathes in deeply and allows himself to tune into what his nerves are telling him to do.

He drops one hand from the steering wheel, keeping a close eye for any reaction. He removes the karambit from its hiding place at his thigh and palms it, tucking it into his sleeve. He then slowly raises his hands, opens his door, and slides out, his empty palms proffered like a gift. Shotgun eyes, black and mirthless, follow his movements, like obedient but unfriendly dogs.

'Sorry, was going a bit too fast,' says Pete mildly. 'Didn't mean to frighten you gents.'

'We ain't frightened,' snaps Zeke. The beating Pete administered the night before burns in his eyes and he has the look of someone with a point to prove.

'I'm just trying to get home,' says Pete. 'Been an emergency. I've got to get back. What's with the guns, gentlemen? I'm not sure that's necessary?'

'We'll decide what's necessary, Mr Collins,' purrs Noah. 'And from what I understand, a gun is absolutely necessary.'

'How is Joe?' says Pete. 'Resting up this morning, I suspect. Rough night...we all have 'em.'

Noah's face drops, suddenly raw and ugly with anger. 'You're lucky I don't shoot you right now, you cocky fucker. If I had my way, you'd be dead in a ditch. Worm food.'

'Doing as you're told, are you? There's a good boy,' says Pete.

Noah's face reddens. 'Just keep your hands up nice and high, Mr Collins, where we can see them,' he says. He nods in the direction of the car. 'Zeke, check his car. Tom, give him a pat down, and don't go getting any ideas, Collins, I'm a good shot, many years of practice.'

The trajectory of every interaction is often set by a few simple facts, think Pete. He must now assume they know who he is. Why else would they have turned up armed to the teeth? The bigger, as yet unresolved question, is what exactly do they want with him? The scarecrow corpses give a pretty strong hint of what awaits him. Half measures won't serve him now. It's full throttle. That said, it occurs to him if they wanted him dead, he would be already. They've had plenty of time to finish him off, they are in the middle of nowhere, and no-one around here is going to react to the distant crack of a shotgun. Which means they just intend to collect him. To take him somewhere else. It is, therefore, a question of timing. Does he back himself to take them down now? A knife against two shotguns and an axe doesn't feel like great odds.

Noah gives him an unpleasantly knowing smile, revealing his scattered yellowing teeth, as if he knows exactly what Pete is thinking.

Zeke is on his knees in the front of his car. 'What've we got here then!!' he cries. He holds up the Glock, like a magician pulling a rabbit from a hat.

'Give it to me, Zeke. I wants to take a look at it,' says Noah greedily. Zeke hands it to him while he balances his shotgun on his arm. 'What's a fella like you doing with a gun like this?' he says with a knowing smirk. 'Not your everyday weapon this, but you're not an everyday fella, are you, Mr Collins?'

Pete says nothing.

'Zeke, see if there's anything else. Look proper. Make sure you don't miss anything.'

Zeke hustles back to the car, fishes around in the back seats momentarily and then pops the boot. He hauls out Pete's rucksack and tosses it on the ground.

'Anything else?' says Noah urgently.

'Just a bag, you want me to look inside?'

'Not yet, Zeke. First, we need to give Mr Collins a once-over,' says Noah. 'Now then, you heard them stories, lads, about them snakes, the ones with big fangs. The venom they make is precious, but to get it is dangerous, so you have to pull their teeth, you take 'em away and it makes 'em weak. That's what we'll do with Mr Collins here. We pull his teeth. But carefully, lads, he's a snake.'

Tom steps towards Pete. He hefts his axe in his hands and looks at Noah uncertainly.

'Set it down, Tom,' says Noah. 'We've got you covered. Mr Collins isn't about to do anything stupid. Not with a couple of shotguns in his face.'

Pete watches Tom approach with a neutral expression. Tom on the other hand has the look of a man who's been asked to put his hand in a nest of hornets. Pete thinks Tom's neck, which is thick and cabled with veins, is an inviting target. He lets the knife drop into his hand. *Fuck it*, he thinks, *there might be better a time, but I'm done with this – time to go to work...*

The knife cuts the air in a neat, economical arc. Neither it nor Pete make a sound, and it all happens very quickly. The blade is horribly sharp, and it makes short work of Tom's windpipe, passing through his throat, cutting short his breath so suddenly he gapes in shocked surprise as blood fountains down his neck and soaks his jumper. He drops to his knees and slumps forward onto his face before Noah even has time to bring his shotgun up.

Pete's already moving. One down is not enough. If he can get to Zeke before Noah reacts, he thinks there's a chance he might be able to deal with all three of them.

Unfortunately, Noah recovers his senses rather quicker than Pete would've liked. He's within striking distance of Zeke, knife taut in his hand, when a shotgun barrel is shoved level with his face. Pete stares down its twin eyes, and Noah's equally black gaze, and realises the moment has passed. He puts his arms out to his sides and makes a show of dropping the knife to the floor.

'What, what's he done to Tom!? Tom, are you...what's wrong with Tom!' shrieks Zeke, his voice high and childlike.

'Tom's dead, Zeke, and so will you be if you don't stop with that screeching,' says Noah. 'Now get your gun on this rotten bastard and stop messing around. He's what I said he was, a nasty bugger, a snake. More than I thought. Gotta keep a good close eye on him, right...'

Zeke points his shotgun at him unsteadily. Whatever orders they had to bring him in, Pete knows he needs to be on his best behaviour, long enough for the fast blood these two are pumping to slow down. Hot heads can override the strictest orders. Pete places his hands behind his head. He beacons calm submission, projecting it on a frequency he hopes these two will pick up. He can hear Zeke's breathing, rapid, like a dog on a hot day.

Noah checks Tom, who is lying face down in the road. An expanding pool of blood creates a midnight halo around his head, even blacker than the asphalt. He gives him a quick once-over. 'He's dead,' he says. 'For now at least.'

'We should kill this fucker right here and now!' shouts Zeke. His lips are flecked with frothy spittle.

'Not yet, Zeke. Not yet,' says Noah. 'Not our place. He'll get what's coming to him. He'll wish he were dead before he does too. Now, let's get Tom up in that back of the Land Rover, can't leave him out here for the crows, can we. Bring it up a bit closer, he's a big lad, and I don't need to put my back out.'

Zeke snarls at Pete as he heads over to the Land Rover. He jumps inside, guns the engine noisily and angrily reverses it to where Tom lies. He is out of the cab before it has even stopped, flinging open the double doors at the rear, revealing a sparse interior with benches bolted to each side and a dirty metal floor between them.

Noah takes a step towards Pete and crashes the butt of his shotgun into Pete's temple. He drops to the floor, out cold.

'Should've done that before,' Noah says to himself. He looks at his friend's dead body. 'Sorry, Tom, we'll get you home, you wait. Tie him up, Zeke. Good and tight. Better check in his pockets to make sure he doesn't have any more surprises for us.'

Zeke roughly checks the pockets of Pete's coat and finds the spare clips for the Glock. He tosses them to Noah. A cursory pat down finds nothing more. 'That's the lot. He's clean,' he says.

He pulls Pete's hands together, wrapping rope a few times around his wrists. Zeke finishes his knot and gives it a vigorous tug, looking for approval from Noah, which he gets in the form of a brisk nod.

They lift Tom's body into the Land Rover, placing him on top of some old fertilizer sacks in between the benches. A pool of blood swiftly forms between the corrugated steel slats. Pete's unconscious body is next, and they prop him up behind the driver's seat. A seat belt is pulled across his chest to hold him upright.

'Zeke, take his car back to the cottage,' says Noah. 'Leave the keys in it. It's a rental so someone's going to come looking for it eventually. We can take it back, hand it over, or maybe just burn it out someplace. I'll check with Margaret. For now dump it there and come back.'

Noah sits himself opposite Pete in the back of the Land Rover. Outside a light rain begins to fall, tip-tapping on the roof.

Pete opens his eyes, just a crack, and winces at the bolt of pain that rips up the side of his face. He moves his jaw gently from side to side, the tendons creaking like rope securing a ship in dock.

'Try that again and I'll kill you...' says Pete.

Noah smiles. 'I think your days of killing are over. There's a whole new world of pain for you to discover, Mr Collins. You're going to wish I'd put a bullet between your eyes.'

Pete wants to cradle his skull, which feels as if it's been split in two, but finds his hands glued to his lap. He contents himself with a gentle shake, which sets off a jangling carousel in his head that leaves him nauseous. He closes his eyes and allows himself to drift on waves of pain.

After an undetermined amount of time, Zeke returns. He clambers into the driver seat and starts the engine. 'Car's all clean. Left it outside the cottage like you said. We ready?' he asks Noah.

'We are, Zeke. Let's go...'

Chapter 12

The mist has returned by the time Ezekiel's Land Rover arrives at the village. He parks it on the road opposite the church, yanks on the handbrake and switches off the ignition. The engine dies with a juddering symphony of phuts and growls. Pete listens to the soft tick of it cooling, a metronome that throbs in time with a lump that is rising on his temple like soft dough.

Noah's said nothing during the ten-minute drive. He just fixes Pete with a blackened gaze, while his hand strokes the barrel of his shotgun like a favoured dog. His grin, framed between cracked lips, is dry and unpleasant. Tom's body lies between them on the floor and the flow of blood from his slashed throat has slowed to a trickle.

Pete tosses limited options back and forth in his head, as if a ball between distracted hands. He's outgunned, until he can be reunited with his Glock, so is inclined to allow this riptide to drag him to its conclusion. Experience tells him it pays not to struggle and waste energy. The tide would weaken at some point and give him up, provided he's patient and doesn't force things.

'We're here,' growls Zeke. 'What now?'

'Time to go, Mr Collins. Some folks want to chat with you. You'll find it educational.'

'I doubt that,' says Pete.

Noah's eyes blacken. 'You need to start listening, instead of yapping. Goddam, I would've enjoyed killin' you. At least I'll get to see you die, cruel. That's something.'

Zeke opens the rear doors. Noah gestures with the shotgun. 'Now get the fuck out,' he says.

The village green has seeded spectators. A small crowd of people watch Pete climb out of the Land Rover. He walks gingerly. The ringing in his skull infects his legs, making them feel like matchsticks. Three men and a woman watch him. Pete thinks he recognises the old lady, she was walking with Penny the other morning. One of the men nods a curt welcome to Noah, who raises a hand in greeting. He calls him over. 'You two, give us a hand with Tom,' he says. 'Grab him. You take his feet, careful now. Take him to Caleb.' They follow his instruction without a word. Neither gives Pete a second look.

Tom's corpse is hoisted out of the Land Rover, like it's the most normal thing in the world to be depositing a dead body at the doors of the local church. Pete's shotgun escort must be equally unremarkable. He's alarmed to think this may well be just another normal morning in Little Baddington.

Noah and Zeke steer Pete towards the churchyard gate. Zeke hasn't poked him in the back with the barrel of his shotgun yet, but Pete can feel his eagerness to do so. The steepled roof above the gate is festooned with more of the horrible corn figures, a Lilliputian court that watches his procession with slitted eyes. He passes under the eaves and sees a new addition to the decorations. Another freshly harvested goat foetus is hung between the branches of the twisted yew tree. It hisses gently in the cool morning air. Noah tugs a forelock in deference when they pass beneath it. Two pallbearers carry Tom's body silently behind them.

Ahead, standing within the shadows of the vestibule, is Father Caleb. He's dressed in a black cassock that settles just above his shoes. Around his neck is a chain and small silver cross. He grins enthusiastically, clapping his hands together, the action childlike and at odds with his shaven-headed countenance.

'Peter!' he cries. 'Welcome! A pleasure to see you again!' He hurries towards him, his cassock swishing about his legs, as if welcoming him to a cocktail party. Tom is carried past and he offers the two pallbearers a sober nod as they head into the church.

He dismisses Noah and Zeke, waving them away as if they're flies hovering around a tasty sandwich. They withdraw but their shotguns remain watchful.

A meaty hand is planted on Pete's shoulder. His grip is persuasive, encouraging him to walk in step with him under the boughs of the yew trees. Noah and Zeke fall into step behind them, their presence signified by the scrunch of gravel on the path.

'Now, I'm sure you're wondering why the chaps came out to collect you this morning. You must have lots of questions, why wouldn't you!? Under the circumstances!' He offers a small, almost apologetic grin. 'You've made yourself some enemies already, haven't you? Poor old Joseph. Luckily, we've managed to reattach his ear, but goodness, aren't you very rough? You are not a man to be taken lightly it seems. Hence the rather over-the-top escort! Now then, lots to discuss. You're wondering what's going on in Little Baddington? All in good time, Peter, all in good time.' He claps his hands together delightedly, and Pete decides that Father Caleb is more than a little mad.

'Come, let us enter God's house and sit for a spell. Before the others arrive. I'll explain what I can, and then, well then we can get on with….' he pauses over his choice of words, lips smacking together like he is tasting something good, 'Things…'

He pushes open the door and they enter Little Baddington's goliath church.

Chapter 13

Father Caleb's hand is a coercive presence on Pete's shoulder as he walks him up the aisle of the church, like a dowry.

Pete spots a streak of crimson on the floor where a misplaced foot has slipped in Tom's blood, but the corpse is nowhere to be seen. His hands are still tied, although Zeke's knot is already loose. He thinks he will be able to get free when it matters but there is no sense telegraphing that advantage, so he continues his pantomime of incarceration.

'I love this place,' breathes Caleb. 'It is….' He pauses, casting an adoring gaze about him. 'Our place. By that I mean it belongs to us all, all of us here in the village, and that's a wonderful thing, is it not? In this day and age, to have a place you can call your own. So important in an increasingly isolating world. A world where it is harder and harder to know where you belong. Well, Peter, here in Little Baddington we've worked hard to create a place we all belong, and that belonging is first vested in the bricks and mortar of this church. It bleeds from every stone, you see. There is sacrifice here, necessary sacrifice, to keep it as we like it, as it needs to be…'

They stop halfway down the rows of pews. Pete reckons the church must have space for least three hundred people, and that's got to be three times what's required, even if the whole village turned up for every service.

'Why are you telling me this?' says Pete. 'And why've you brought me here?'

'Peter, don't do me the disservice of pretending you don't know why you're here,' says Caleb. His smile doesn't reach his eyes, which have hardened like flint. 'Your hands itch for a knife, or maybe a gun? Don't they? I can see it. Feel it even.'

Pete looks towards the door, where Noah and Zeke stand guard.

'There's nowhere for you to go. Give yourself a break, take a breath. Don't think foolish thoughts, not here. For they are mine to see, praise thanks to the glory of our Lord,' says Caleb. He casts his hand towards the pulpit, and the statute of the goat god, which broods over the pews like a jealous lover. The stained glass is lit by the morning light. It reveals a crucifixion, in all its bloody glory, albeit with one adjustment. The splayed figure of Christ has a goat's head, its eyes slitted, horns spiralling away from its skull, which is cracked into a feral grin.

'Ah, the sunlight grants you a vision of our adjustment. Just a little twist on an oh-so-familiar scene, Peter. Isn't it wonderful! That is the face of our true Lord and saviour, as you will see...' says Caleb. His face shines with reverence. 'But first, let us sit for a spell and talk. I'm not a man who likes secrets, they are the rot of a soul, are they not? I must share one with you, it itches at me, and it's time to set it free...'

Caleb gestures to a pew in the shadow of the pulpit. He guides Pete to sit and deposits himself next to him. He crosses his legs with some difficulty, prissily rearranging his cassock. 'I'm going to tell you something you might not like very much. But before I do, I'd like to check that you've have had your fangs fully pulled. Not because I don't trust you or anything, your hands are tied after all, but I'd just feel a bit more comfortable that a man like you isn't armed. I only have my faith to protect me after all, so it's only fair I make sure we have a level playing field.'

He whistles and his dogs do his bidding.

'He's clean, Father,' says Zeke. 'I checked him myself.'

'Was that before or after he killed Tom?' says Caleb coldly. 'Check him again.'

Noah places the eye of his shotgun on Pete's forehead. 'He's a lamb, Father. Don't worry. He's done messing around.'

'I don't know who you think I am,' says Pete. 'I'm just on holiday. That's all.'

'Sshh now,' says Caleb. 'Please, let us end this charade. I know who you are, Pete Collins, I even know that's not your real name. I know you, and more importantly I know what you are. That is, after all, the reason why you've have found your way to my door...'

Caleb breaks into a dry chuckle.

'You're here for salvation, even if you don't know it yet, as are all of your kind...'

'My kind?' says Pete.

'Yes, your kind,' says Caleb with relish. He punches Pete playfully on the arm. 'You are a killer, are you not? A dealer of death, for the right price? Stealing the Lord's divine gift, his divine right, and making it your own? You harvest souls, untethering them, so they might walk into the arms of the Lord? What a gift that is.' He pauses, aware that he is falling into the inescapable rhythm of tub-thumping bible bashers the world over. 'They do not find salvation,' he says quietly, his tone forced conversational now, steeped in a faux regret. 'They have died an unnatural death. They belong to you. Because of what you have done, taker of souls. As now for poor Tom, a father, a husband, a son. The latest victim of your unnatural ministrations.'

'It isn't personal. It never is...' says Pete.

'Ha! You would say that. It matters not. I said that we look after our own here in Little Baddington? Tom will find benefit, if it is our Lord's will.' He sees Pete's puzzled expression and waves it away. 'All will be revealed, be patient,' he says. 'Building this sanctuary was far from easy. The outside world is eager to stamp over the traditions of the countryside, of the people who were born and raised on this soil. The outsiders are everywhere you see, with their big money and their big houses. They grow in number every year, squeezing themselves in without thought for what they are squeezing out, the quaint cottage that housed a family of farmhands for generations, the little shop that served a community and now sells avocados for a king's ransom, the roads that don't fit their great big cars, the pub that serves a plate of food for the price of feeding a family for a week. They don't see the hard work, and hardship that's held up these thatched roofs and laid the honey-coloured stone. They don't know how our schools, once full of joyous local voices, are now silent. How empty a village becomes, when neighbours are replaced with locked doors, how the people that remain wither in that emptiness.... In Little Baddington we cried enough! Enough! It was time to take back what we have and preserve it.' Caleb pauses. He removes a handkerchief from his pocket and wipes it across a sweaty brow. 'And so,' he says, quietly now, 'that is what we have done, we have created an oasis of yesterday amidst the torrid whirlwind of today. A place that outsiders cannot ruin. A place for locals. All at the behest of our god, provided we furnish him with what he wants.

'What does your god want?' says Pete.

'Why, what all gods crave, ultimately…. Sacrifice!' says Caleb. 'You are familiar with the phrase, the blacker the berry, the sweeter the fruit? As it is for souls. The blacker the better, and yours, yours, my friend, is a black as midnight in hell, whether you like it or not…' He smiles as the butt of Noah's shotgun reacquaints itself with Pete's head.

Pete sees only darkness.

Chapter 14

As anyone who's taken a heavy blow to the head will tell you, there's a big difference between waking up and coming around.

Pete's skull reverberates like a tuning fork as he breaks the surface of unconsciousness and takes a ragged breath in the now. The pulse in his head is the sickly swirl of a carousel. He coughs weakly and hears a taunting echo.

His predicament hasn't improved. He's no longer in the church, insofar as he can tell. It's pitch black, so dark he feels its oppressive weight on his eyeballs as he seeks out even a pinprick of light that might help him orientate himself. His hands are tied, but are now fastened at head height, his arms stretched out at right angles as if crucified. His ankles are bound together. By shifting his weight, he manages a small movement in either direction but nothing more. He feels grit under his back, and the air smells old, as if he's in a cellar.

Pete snares his racehorse heart. The solid blackness feels like purgatory, but one he's sharing with someone else. He hears laboured breathing, slow and regular, like someone is sleeping. If they are, they are troubled by nightmares, as the silence is spiked by a childlike whimpering.

After a time, he hears different noises. The shuffle of footsteps, the murmur of low conversation. There is a clank of an opening lock, followed by a blast of light. Pete sees an arched stone ceiling above him. The brickwork is ancient and crumbling, festooned with spiderweb stalactites. He turns his head to the right and sees who's been keeping him company. It's Craig. He is also bound to a rough stone altar. He's blindfolded and there's a cloth gag pushed into his mouth.

Beyond, he sees stone steps hewn into a wall. Pete's restricted line of sight reveals shoes that grow legs and then bodies, as one after another people descend into the crypt beneath Little Baddington church.

'Peter!' cries Caleb, 'You're awake! How wonderful.'

Caleb is followed by a dutiful procession of villagers. Pete recognises Noah and Joe. Joe carries a rough hessian sack on his shoulder. Behind them walks Margaret. Her grey hair is drawn into a tight bun, her face severe, with bloodless lips and pale watery eyes. Maria and Herschel descend next, grim-faced. At the rear is a lady Pete hasn't seen before. She's younger, with straw-coloured hair. She stands between two small children, who each carry a wicker basket. They look like the kids he saw in his waking dream on the train to Moreton-in-Marsh. They have flat faces and empty eyes, but smile dreamily, as if on a delightful school outing.

Margaret shoots Pete an amused glance. She busies herself lighting candles that are positioned around the walls. The crypt reveals itself amidst the flickering candlelight.

There is a third stone altar to Pete's left. It isn't obvious how its occupant is going to contribute to proceedings. It's Tom. His corpse sprawls untethered on the stone, his slashed throat snarling at Pete like an accusation. Immediately in front of him, there is a fourth and final altar, situated at the centre of the crypt. It's more decorative; someone has woven yew branches around it, which spiral upwards as if sprouting from the dusty floor, forming an eagle's nest at its top.

Margaret lights candles that sit either side of this nest. 'Well, Mr Collins,' she says softly. 'You're in a spot of bother, aren't you?'

Joe drops his hessian sack at the base of the nest. He smirks at Pete, but his face is pale and betrays an underlying fear. He re-joins Noah, who stands with Maria and Herschel.

Craig moans beneath his gag. No-one pays him any attention.

Caleb approaches. 'You'll enjoy this, Peter,' he says. 'You're about to witness something truly spectacular, something very few people are privileged to see...'

Caleb hoists up the sack and carefully tips its contents onto the top of the altar. A slick pinkish body pours onto it with a greasy thump. Another embryonic goat, harvested from Little Baddington's seemingly endless supply. He steps back quickly, as if he might get burnt. He tosses the sack into the corner of the crypt.

Caleb rests a distracted hand on Craig's leg, giving it a gentle pat. Craig's moans intensify. 'Sshh, there,' he says softly. 'Not much longer now.' He returns his gaze to Pete, bright-eyed and eager, like a teacher bursting to impart knowledge.

'You're wondering what's happening?' He laughs, its edges jagged with hysteria. 'It has been quite a day already! How is your head, not too sore, I hope? I'm counting two or maybe even three raps to the skull? My apologies, on behalf of us all. We are civilised folk, as far as we can be, and I personally abhor unnecessary violence.' He pauses, savouring his thoughts as if a fine wine. His congregation, though small, listens raptly.

'You are our special guest and so deserve a full explanation.' He leans over him, his face aglow. 'You will bear witness to the mechanism by which we secure our peace. It has been a journey. I don't expect you to understand. It has taken time for many in the village to understand it, but now we are united in our beliefs. You see, Peter, we have little need for an all-seeing God here, not anymore. A God that doesn't understand our suffering, one that is too removed from the coalface of life, is not useful to us. The Christian Church, bless its dusty good intentions, it thinks prayer and stoicism will solve all the ills that infect modern life. You and I know that's no truer now than it ever was. We need a more.... specific god, one that has our interests at heart, that listens to our woes and addresses them if in its wisdom it sees fit. A local god, if you will. Observe, Peter...It will be an education, I think.'

Pete hears a few muttered amens.

Caleb turns to Craig, placing a hand on his chest, over his beating heart. Craig flaps around like a landed fish in response, his muffled screams finding gaps in the cloth gag and reverberating around the walls.

'This soul came from the outside. He stole our public house from right under our noses. A mistake. Our patron, dear Lord Baddington, is not the man he was. We're careful with our property, it does not find its way into the hands of outsiders, but this time, well, his children, that greedy, covetous progeny, they placed sticky fingers into his head. The clerical error that followed will be rectified, but now it's time for Craig to pay his dues. Unlike his lovely wife, he's not made any effort to fit in. Regretful. Penny will mourn him, but only briefly, I think. She's part of the village now.'

Caleb produces a knife from his pocket. It's Pete's karambit and its blade gleams yellow in the flickering candlelight.

'Suited to the job in hand. You've taken care of your tools, Peter, as any good craftsman should. Herschel's confident it'll do the trick, aren't you, Herschel. He's familiar with a carcass, skinned more than a few in his time, so no reason to think this'll be any different!' he finishes brightly.

Pete's stomach lurches. 'You're all mad,' he says.

'Of course we are,' says Caleb, his face suddenly serious. 'It pays to be a little mad these days. It is a mad world, after all. Ask your friends up in London? They don't care what we do, or why we do it, just that we do it.'

'You're fucking lunatics!' says Pete. His head suddenly feels as if it's been stuffed with explosives.

'Calm, Peter, be calm. I said we have secrets. We know your 'Dave', and the people he serves. Surely you know there's no honour amongst thieves. The service we offer is simple. Like magicians we make problems disappear. It pays handsomely, in so many ways. Mutually beneficial is the phrase, I think.'

Caleb hands the knife to Herschel, who busily removes his coat. He rolls up the sleeves of his shirt runs a hand through his bushy moustache and contemplates the work ahead.

Chapter 15

A human nervous system only has a finite level of tolerance. At some point fuses blow and the lights go out. Pete's borne witness to many deaths in his life, mostly at his own hand. He has, however, avoided unnecessary suffering, even when more twisted instructions specifically requested it. A clean death was simpler, less unusual, and so less likely to arouse suspicion. It's an approach that'd served him well for many years, up until his mistake with Archibald Hunter.

They did things differently in Little Baddington.

Craig's screams fade to weak gurgling splutters. Herschel is in the process of peeling his skin from his torso, as if he is skinning a fish. Craig is, technically at least, alive, but blessed unconsciousness has folded him into its embrace. Herschel continues his work quietly, save for an occasional grunt of effort when he shifts the body to get better access for his knife. Once removed, Craig's skin is roughly folded, looking like dirty laundry, and presented to Caleb, who places it reverentially on top of the dead goat on the altar.

'Ah, God's work, it's hard, but so rewarding,' says Caleb with a smile.

'Amen,' grunts Herschel.

'Fuck me,' croaks Pete, who's processing the confirmation that Dave's sending failed contract killers to the Cotswolds where they're ritually sacrificed.

'Nearly there, Peter. A few more contributions, and then Craig's played his part. Bless him and all he gives to the furrows.'

'Bless our Lord in the furrows,' chimes the congregation from the shadows.

Caleb nods at Herschel. He places the karambit next to Craig. The altar's awash with thick blood; it shines black in the candlelight. The air is metallic with it, harsh and coppery at the back of Pete's throat. Herschel collects another knife, this one longer, with a heavier blade. He looks to Caleb for instruction.

'Brothers and sisters, it's time for new life! Let this callow soul's heartbeat pass, let it grow strong in the chest of our Lord, where it will beat with renewed purpose and vigour. Let it do so for the mercy of our Lord in the furrows...'

'In the furrows,' they chime as Herschel's knife flashes down into Craig's chest. There is a crack as it breaks through his chest plate. He sets to work, his grunts of effort louder now as he fishes around within Craig's broken chest. Fresh slick blood plasters his arms, as he lifts out a wobbling, vaguely pulsating heart. He hands it to Caleb, who holds it above his head. Blood runs down his arms and splatters his face. He places it on top of the folds of skin.

'Blessed is our Lord, we now offer eyes so he may see!' he cries.

Margaret steps forward. Pete had a feeling she wouldn't be missing out on all the fun. She shoots Pete an amused look. She has what looks like a spoon in each hand, only these spoons taper to a sharpened point. The edge catches the candlelight and winks, like it's imparting a secret. Margaret takes her place, hovering over Craig's head.

'In the furrows,' they cry and Margaret starts to fish around in Craig's eye sockets. It looks as if she's done this before, it takes only a moment for her to offer an eyeball to Caleb. It sits on the spoon like a punctured poached egg, bleeding crimson yolk. Craig's deflated eyeballs are deposited on top of the heart. One slides off onto the stone with a meaty plop.

'And now, dear Peter, your moment. It is time for a little contribution from you. In lieu of what will come more fulsomely in due course,' says Caleb. 'Margaret – are we ready?'

'We are indeed,' says Margaret. She pours melted wax into a copper bowl. It's placed over a flame, where it bubbles softly.

'Joseph,' says Caleb. 'Come forward, brother, you doubtless have something to say to our guest.'

Joe's taken the long blade from Herschel. He stands over Pete, smiling. 'Not laughing now, are you,' he says softly.

'Are you left- or right-handed, Peter?' says Caleb. 'Probably both? I think we'll take your right. The one that stole Tom's breath, and poor Joe's ear. Only fair...'

Joe brings the knife whistling down. Its razor edge crunches through skin and bone, severing Pete's forearm. The blade rings against the stone. Margaret is quickly at his side, she presses cloth against the fountaining stump, binding it, before plunging it into the bubbling bowl of wax. Pete screams, pulling taut against the ropes that hold him in place. A gag is stuffed into his mouth.

'Come to us, oh Lord,' cries Caleb. 'He who walks in the furrows, we bring you skin, and heart, and hand, and eyes to see. Come to us once again.'

The crypt darkens perceptibly, as if a cloud passes over winter sun. The candles flicker amidst new and unknown breezes that are born within the yew branches that cradle the altar. They rustle secretly, building in strength. The candles extinguish as one. One of the children whimpers but is hushed into silence. Caleb's congregation becomes a collective intake of breath.

Something has joined them in the darkness of the crypt. Pete hears mewling sounds and thick porridgy movement. The insanity of the moment is overwhelming. Despite the screaming agony of his stump, he strains against his bindings in the darkness. He hears footsteps around him. Margaret is relighting the candles. Shadows dance across the vaulted ceiling in rhythm with cries of exaltation from Caleb and his congregation. Pete doesn't want to see what is moving on the altar. He doesn't want to see what Caleb has conjured into this room, which is suddenly icy cold, freezing the sweat on his back.

Backlit by candlelight and dressed in shadows, a vaguely humanoid form is rising from within the nest of branches. It grows inexorably, thickening in sinew, cracking burgeoning bones into place as it races from embryonic to adolescent. It reminds Pete of the old stop motion animations that chased Sinbad and terrified him as a child. Every inch of him is focused on flight, his heels find purchase in the altar and he levers himself up, tearing skin bound by ropes, the pain a hissing white noise when compared to the horror that rises in front of him.

Caleb is suddenly next to him. He places a hand on Pete's shoulder. 'Hush now, Peter, do not fear. For he is a beautiful and benevolent god. He is our god; he is for us and of us. Watch. For he has miracles to share.'

The creature peels itself off the altar, stepping down on elongated legs that sprout coarse hair. It wavers, snakelike in movement, and the light picks up a heavily muscled torso. Its flesh is ragged, but stolen skin knits together, as if under the hand of a magical tailor. Its eyes reflect the dancing flame of the candles. They are wide and set either side of a broad misshaped skull. The pupils are rectangular and unmistakably goat-like.

'Behold, child of Baphomet. Keeper of the Furrows. Keeper of Little Baddington...'

It steps forward and the congregation collapse into babbling worship. The young mother drops to her knees and wails. Her two children grasp each other's hands and watch, stony-faced.

Margaret stands beside Caleb, her face in rapture as he prostrates himself before it. Pete sees sweat on his broad skull despite the drop in temperature within the crypt. His body is reverb and terror is peppered within his words.

'We serve you, oh Lord, welcome back to the furrows,' he cries.

It cocks its great head at Caleb. Nubs at the side of its skull burst through skin, growing into twisted horn. Its eyes betray nothing, their goat-like provenance denies even a hint of humanity. Caleb feels it too, thinks Pete, as he seems to shrivel in the presence of his god. He wonders if any of them even begin to understand the deal that's been struck to keep Little Baddington for the locals. If gods exist above and below, Pete's money is on this one coming from the latter.

'Dear Lord, with whom we are blessed to speak. We ask in your name, to offer favour to one of your trip, who has suffered for you. He was young and strong, and a faithful servant. He carries seed that will grow your trip and we beg you return him to us...' Caleb gestures to Tom's corpse, and the goat god's gaze follows his direction. It looks at Pete, and its head tips quizzically, a motion Pete finds bizarrely human.

'All you see is yours, my Lord, but first...we beg...' says Caleb, motioning towards Tom's corpse.

The goat god stares blankly in reply, its countenance oozes displeasure and the temperature in the crypt plummets further towards arctic. It turns and walks on cloven feet towards Tom's corpse. It sniffs deeply, making hungry clucking noises deep in its throat.

'No, my Lord, not to feed, my Lord, to restore. For he was faithful in the furrows,' says Caleb.

The child of Baphomet frowns, and then starts to retch with increasing violence until eventually it spews thick black bile onto Tom's pale upturned face. Margaret rushes forward, opens up Tom's mouth and allows the thick liquid to pour into his throat. What remains is scooped into a bowl and placed reverentially to one side.

The god has tottered back to its birth altar. Whatever it's just done has exhausted it. Margaret helps it back onto the altar, where it folds its legs under itself, like a foal, and curls into sleep. 'Rest, my Lord, rest,' she says softly.

Tom suddenly awakens. He heaves in gasping breath; colour flushes his grey skin, and he rolls onto his side coughing weakly. Brackish liquid, the colour of autumnal decay, spills from his mouth. The crypt is filled with a sickening stench. Pete thinks of drains unblocked, of slick dead things flushed out into the light. The young woman and children run to him, throwing arms around his shivering frame, crying exaltations.

'See!' says Caleb. 'See what he does! He returns our brother to us, back into the furrows.' His eyes shine. 'Take Thomas back to your family, Lucille, deep in praise of our Lord, He who walks in the furrows.' Noah helps Tom off the altar. Lucille fusses around him, cooing like a dove, and he is swallowed into the arms of his family.

'Caleb,' says Margaret sharply. 'We are done. Go home, all of you, we'll have work tonight, but for now our Lord must rest.' The congregation is obedient and files up the stairs leaving the crypt silent, save for muted grunts and snores emanating from the yew nest where the creature sleeps.

'Quite the morning, Mr Collins,' says Margaret, her tone forced conversational. 'Quite the morning....' She runs a hand along the altar, giving Pete's ropes a cursory shake and inspects his stump. The wax has hardened, searing the wound as she'd hoped. 'A bit harder to tie you up now. Your stump's not got the same purchase as a wrist.' She smiles, as if she's sharing a pun over drinks. 'The bleeding's stopped. Mostly at least. You'll be good for a few hours yet. And let's be honest, that's all you've got left anyway.' She barks laughter that bounces back off the walls.

'It's not Caleb's village, you know,' she says softly. 'It's mine. It's always been mine. My father ran this place, he was the vicar, long before Caleb.' She laughs again. 'He'd spent much of his life studying the bible, learning the word of God. It broke him when he found it wanting. Empty. When he realised the promises he made were not delivered, his parishioners were not saved. So what is a noble man to do? When he sees the world he fashioned crumbling around him, the deep bites being taken from all he knew? And what is a daughter to do when she sees the father she loves more than anything in the world despair at his impotence in the face of so-called progress? I'll tell you. A daughter studies. She develops special interests. She reads words to the left and right of the bible, the words that run underneath that 'holy' text. She discovers a different type of holy. A better kind, one that delivers on its promises, one that understands the reality of contract, of buyer and seller. My father cried *caveat emptor*! But he was in awe of his good daughter. He saw the light, so to speak. We made our choice, between reality and the empty promises of a dead religion, and now we flourish. Safe in the furrows.'

'If I get out of here, I'm going to kill you. All of you,' croaks Pete.

Margaret laughs softly.

'Even if you could make good on your empty threats, haven't you seen the power we have at our disposal? Have your eyes been so closed? Death is the least of our worries in Little Baddington. Eternal life belongs to us .... Real eternal life, not the metaphorical kind. I am older than I appear, much older, as are many of us. What revived Thomas, can also hold us steady, it stops the clocks chiming, the hour hand does not move. So hold your tongue, so wastefully full of idle chatter. Sit tight, Mr Collins, I'll be back later. Enjoy being in the presence of our

Lord. He who walks in the furrows. It is truly an honour... You're never leaving Little Baddington. Put that thought to rest. It's easier if you accept it. It's the hope that kills you, after all.'

She gives Pete a sympathetic pat on his shoulder. It has all the sincerity of a knife in the back. With a final adoring glance at the sleeping creature, she departs. A door shuts softly. Pete hears the clunk of a latch, but not the turn of a key.

Hope doesn't kill, thinks Pete. *But I do.*

Chapter 16

Time moves glacially slow in the presence of true fear. Each and every second draws out like a blade, and on those sharpened edges rational thought is severed, leaving only maggoty, rotten ones, the ones that live below, deep in the primal mirk that ferments our nightmares.

Pete is listening to the harsh rise and fall of the sleeping chest of a god. The day has added a lifetime of nightmare fuel to his already healthy tank, but witnessing the birth of a demon, followed by a vomit-induced resurrection of a corpse is beyond even his capacity.

He stares over his toes at a bestial shadow that rises and falls in time with the ragged breathing of the child of Baphomet. The candles have grown stubby, promising darkness. The thought of sharing the darkness with what occupies the altar is not a good one.

He's been unable to apply any pressure to the rope that binds his right arm without setting off explosions in his stump, which throbs horribly underneath its wax cap. Instead, Pete concentrates his efforts on the hope offered by the small amount of give in the one that pins down his left hand. The altar is cast from rough stone. He thinks he can work the rope against it, applying steady downward pressure, so it might begin to fray. It is painfully slow work and the rasping sound of rope on stone seems as loud as a chainsaw to his ears. The rope is belligerent, but not it seems, infallible. After an age, it starts to relent, spitting fibres like fireworks. Pete feels the tension at his wrist ease. Hope opens a window in his chest that makes him double his efforts.

His enthusiasm for the task dims his radar. Baphomet's child has woken and it's only when Pete notices a shadow pass across the vaulted ceiling that he realises his folly.

The goat god has grown while it sleeps. It fills the crypt with its shadow. Its breathing is slow and bovine. It snorts the air as it approaches. Pete can do little but pray, which he does in the oddly inconsistent way of atheists the world over, an avalanche of thoughts and promises to no god in particular, mainly to himself and others, to do better, to be better, if he makes it out of this godforsaken place. The god carries the night with it, bringing dank thoughts that infect his head, filling it with whispering nightmares, some familiar, some borrowed. All hellish. The candles waver in unison and the crypt flickers in and out of darkness. His skin prickles as the creature draws near and Pete retreats behind his eyelids, squeezing them shut.

After a moment he hears the unmistakable sound of feeding, the crunching of sinew and bone as Craig's cooling body serves a secondary purpose. He prays his corpse offers enough sustenance to sate the appetite of a god.

****

Evening draws in, pulling darkness across the rooftops of Little Baddington as if to shade the village from external scrutiny. The residents are busy. Margaret conducts an orchestra of activity as they prepare for a night of ritual.

The roads into Little Baddington are secured. The collapse of the bridge means there's one way in, and one way out, by road at least, and so the village is pleasingly inaccessible, a place steeped in inconvenience, and that suits them very well. A couple of men have been dispatched to guard the road, to stop anyone getting in and disturbing proceedings.

Privacy is a prerequisite on nights such as this one, thinks Margaret, when things tend to get a little bloody.

Her breath plumes in the cold air and she rubs her hands together briskly. The night sky is clear, and the grass already scrunches pleasingly under the soles of her shoes. She thinks it will be a fine evening. One the whole village can enjoy. The rituals will help bind them together for another season, strengthening them for the winter that follows All Hallows' Eve.

Her thoughts turn to her prize safely tied up in the crypt of his church. Her arrangement with the criminal underworld predates Caleb. He's missed the years of famine. Insularity was a blessing, but its maintenance was a curse. The village grew thin. Its population dwindled. Choosing between believers and non-believers became more nuanced. The selection of someone within the community suitable for culling became hard. Her father lacked the appetite for it. He was a fundamentally good man, not motived by grievance, real or perceived. Margaret, on the other hand, has no such scruples, and was perfectly content with an internal cull if that was what was required. For her there was always someone suitable, someone who didn't pull their weight, someone who deserved it. Village meetings under her tenure became booby-trapped, paranoia stifling discourse, creating a paralysed orthodoxy born of fear.

Initially the thorny problem of selection was avoided by a decision to pivot to outsiders, but it swiftly became apparent that there were only so many lone hikers, tourists and passers through who could be safely disappeared, without drawing the kind of attention they would struggle to deal with. Little Baddington was isolated, but not that isolated. An alternative source was required.

And so a pipeline was established, direct from the godless cesspits of London, dispensing human souls ripe for sacrifice. Their god was no longer hungry and restless. It was sated and it shared its benevolence with the village, keeping them secure, keeping them alive long past due.

Peter Collins would give his soul to that noble cause this night.

She allows her gaze to wander across the green, over her faithful flock, up the road to The Yew Tree Inn, which is bathed in soft light. She briefly wonders if Penny awaits Craig's return. Or if she knows in her heart that he has gone. *No matter,* she thinks, dismissing sentiment as easily as breadcrumbs from a vest. *The village is all, the village is everything. Penny could be part of that future, or she can help fuel it, the choice is simple…*

'Margaret!'

Father Caleb appears at her side. His face is flushed. The rituals have a habit of restoring vigour to those who participate, she thinks, it's part of the intoxication. 'The stage is set. It will need a blessing, to break the ground for our Lord's steps, but other than that, the night is ours.'

Margaret smiles, revealing neat white teeth. 'I'm very excited, Father. This one's going to be special.'

He pats her on a bony shoulder and walks across the green. Margaret allows him his moment of patronising approval. Caleb needs occasional correction, to remind him of who's really in charge, but tonight of all nights she will forgive him his small indiscretion.

A wooden stage has been built around the maypole. The pole has been strung with razor wire. Noah tests the strength of each wire, of which there are five in total. He wears heavy work gloves, leaning into each strand making them sing softly in the night breeze, a tinkling sound like breaking glass. The razor wire is viciously sharp, as it needs to be, given its intended purpose.

Maria and Herschel light torches that have been placed around the perimeter of the green. A small crowd is gathering.

Joseph leads a pair of floppy-eared goats across the grass. They are heavily pregnant and waddle slowly through the crowd. He flicks at the straggler's plump rear with a stick, and it brays loudly in response, eliciting warm smiles from those watching. The night has the feel of carnival.

Caleb opens his arms wide. 'It has been a long summer, brothers and sisters, but the spirit of our village has endured!' he cries. 'We have prevented the greedy eye of those outside from extending its covetous glance over our honey-coloured cottages, our rambling gardens. This haven is forever local!'

There is a ripple of enthusiastic applause. 'All praise he who walks in the furrows...!' cries Doc Brown, who stands near the front of the crowd. His chant is taken up by the rest.

'Is here OK, Father?' says Joseph. He has led the glassy-eyed goats to the maypole. His hand ruffles one of their tousled heads with affection.

'That's fine, Joseph,' says Caleb. 'Tie them to the pole, they'll be happy there. And how are you, feeling better, I hope? You've had the first taste of justice, more will follow...'

Joseph nods. A hand strays to his heavily bandaged ear. 'Noah says it's been a hard year,' he says. 'Crops have been poor. His Lordship's ill and nowt makes him better, no shooting, birds wasted. He's worried about what might come next...we all are.' Joseph wrings his hands in a way that Caleb finds faintly annoying. He reminds himself of his responsibility, to be the shepherd, to tend his flock; sometimes that requires the lash, sometimes something more gently.

'All is well, Joe. Don't worry. What we've set in place remains. We are strong.' He places a hand on his shoulder, giving it a squeeze. 'You and your brother are rocks in this community. Hold your hand firm this night, do as I ask, and we have a glorious year ahead, safe in the furrows...' The strain in Joseph's face eases. He offers Caleb a grim smile.

'Safe in the furrows,' he says.

Joseph wanders back to his beloved goats, clucking low in his throat. They bleat in reply.

Caleb's smile fades. It is getting harder. The tides that sweep the outside world closer to their door are growing stronger. More and more of the lands around them have fallen to the waves of money that swept out from London, from those that eyed new territory to conquer. Gentrification it was called, steeped in arrogance that there was an inherent improvement in the displacement of all that had happily existed in the absence of high-priced restaurants, of Farrow & Ball paintwork, of Hunter wellies.

Not here, he thinks. *We will endure, with the power of our faith and the will of our god...and with sacrifice, of course...*

****

Pete's not sure if he passed out, fell asleep or simply lost his mind for a few moments. He favours the latter, given the circumstances.

The creature returns to its altar, its appetite sated. Its snores are now bovine and contented, the sound of a stable at midnight, if that stable belonged to the devil himself. The child of Baphomet has eaten well. Craig's ribs have been stripped clean, as if chicken bones on a starving man's plate. His head remains, but the face has been chewed off, leaving a deep bowl where his eyes and nose were. His ponytail hangs apologetically over the side of the stone plinth.

Pete's neck creaks like a rusted weathervane as he rotates his gaze to the sleeping giant before him. And a giant it has become. The food it's eaten has instant effect, swelling muscle and sinew, engorging bone, thickening hair, restoring vigour with its consumption.

When it wakes again, Pete's under no illusion as to what's next on the menu.

The rope that binds his left hand is now worn to threads. He throws his weight against it and continues the seesaw motion that he prays will set him free.

Chapter 17

Ezekiel Benedict, Zeke to his friends, sits in one of the hard-backed pews nearest the door to the crypt. The seat is straight-backed and belligerently uncomfortable, reminding Zeke of school days for some reason, evoking a gloomy mix of tedium and discomfort, all wrapped up with the certainty of punishment. The memory is an unhappy one. As a boy, and now as a man, he wasn't built for discipline. He shared some DNA with Joseph in that respect, and his attendance at the village school had enjoyed the same volatile half-life as the twin brothers. The smell of chalk dusk still makes him feel sick.

He eyes the crypt's heavy wooden door nervously. He's never had the privilege of seeing what was down there. Only a select few of the village have, it was a dowry reserved for Margaret's inner circle, with the promise of admission hung in front of the rest of them, like the proverbial carrot to the donkey.

Zeke's not sure he'd go down even if he was invited. He's thinking about how Tom was a corpse when he was taken there a few hours back, and a sprightlier version of that corpse walked out with his family a short while ago. His old friend's eyes had been wild, like he had witnessed something that had sent him the far side of crazy and he'd not yet fully returned. There was no recognition of the sickly smile he offered when he walked past. It was like smiling at a dead carp.

Zeke and the rest of village have learned to live with the darker stuff, the stuff that made you want to check the locks on your door at night. Margaret and Father Caleb, they delivered on their promises. They were keeping the village safe from outsiders. There was no way that Zeke would be able to afford to live in his cottage, to hope that one day he might find someone to share it with him, on his modest wage, absent of the dark power they'd harnessed. If that meant that occasionally he had to get his hands dirty, well so be it, he thinks. Folks did a lot worse for a lot less, at least that's what Noah says anyway, and Noah is wicked smart.

Zeke trusts Noah the way a sheepdog enjoys the hard hand of its master. His loyalty is absolute. Noah says sometimes it's just easier to do as you're told, to let others make the big decisions, like how the Germans ended up becoming Nazis. Zeke didn't quite follow that one, but it'd made sense when Noah said it.

Zeke's fine with not understanding. He knows he's a blunt instrument, designed for simple tasks. He's more than happy to leave the thinking to others. He'd do as he was told, hold the keys to his little house tightly in his fist, and try not to think about how Tom looks like one of those creatures you see in late-night movies.

The light has dimmed in the church and the big stained-glass window no longer glows. Instead, it casts animalistic shapes that creep across the floor and make Zeke's hair stand up on the back of his neck. He white-knuckles his shotgun, its cold steel not as reassuring as he wants it to be. He wishes they had let someone stay with him, to guard the crypt.

****

Freedom is a gasp of air in a vacuum, a flash of light in the darkness.

It is also the electric twang of a rope twine splintering.

Pete's calcified body warms into life. His left hand is free. He calls calm down from the heavens and cloaks himself within its embrace. The last of the guttering light afforded by the candles allows his eyes to plot a route across the room and up the staircase. He unpicks the rope that holds his stump, wincing as he shuffles across his plinth and does the same to the knots at his ankles. He drops numb legs to the floor, willing blood to refill hungry capillaries.

His knife, its grip tacky with blood, is on the altar that houses Craig's remains. He snatches it up and tucks it inside his belt. Tom's axe is leant against the wall. He picks that up too, distressed at how unbalanced he feels without his right hand. The steel head of the axe catches on the rough floor, and he freezes for a second, his heart stumbling around his chest like a drunk at last orders.

The fear he feels is uncharacteristic, an alien presence that must be controlled, or at least channelled if he's going to survive the day. He snares it, separates the head from the neck and uses that momentum to propel him up the staircase. He doesn't look at the god. He doesn't see its eyes open in the darkness or hear its low growl of displeasure. He thinks about the world above ground, where knives and guns and axes can still solve problems. It is the world he knows and willingly embraces.

****

Zeke doesn't hear the soft creak of the crypt door opening. His propensity for boredom gets the better of him, as he fiddles with his shotgun, attention focused on it instead of his job.

Pete opens the door as if the devil was on his tail, which is exactly how he feels. The time for absolute caution has passed, at least until he's out of the crypt, and then out of this godforsaken village. He spies good ole' Zeke sitting with his back to him, displaying all the guarding credentials he would expect of a countryside bully.

He tests the heft of the axe in his left hand. It feels good, better than he expected. His heart rate drops, and he moves soundlessly across the stone floor.

Zeke's head is removed from his shoulders. It hits the floor with a sodden thump. Zeke's eyes roll up to white, but not before they give Pete an incredulous 'what the fuck!' look even as the head flops across the aisle and settles under the pews. His shotgun clatters to the floor from his suddenly limp fingers and his body falls between the pews where his severed neck fountains blood.

Pete rolls his shoulders, unknotting muscle frozen by his time in the crypt. Zeke is dead and that's fine. The question of whether he deserved it is for another day, and he doesn't expect that day will ever come.

It's time to trade up weaponry. Pete picks up Zeke's shotgun, manages to break it one-handed, and sees the green eyes of two unspent cartridges. He flicks it shut with a satisfying click that is mimicked in the echoing rafters of the church. He frisks Zeke's body, finds a few spare cartridges, and pockets them. Every movement is harder with only one hand. Recalibrating a lifetime of subconscious grace is going to be difficult. He knows there are going to be a lot of folks outside of the church doors. Freedom will require him to dispatch of a good number of them. Four shotgun cartridges and an axe aren't going to be nearly enough. He pines for his Glock.

Time remains his enemy. The church offers false tranquillity. It has long betrayed its heritage as a sanctuary, now offering only a restless demon below his feet and a mob of pseudo-Satanists about it. If he's going to survive the night, he's got to create unstoppable momentum, starting now.

He heads back to the crypt door and sees if he can secure the lock, but is left disappointed; the key for the lock is missing, presumably tucked away in Margaret's pocket. He's pretty sure a god can find its way around a locked door if it wants to, so he wastes no further time on it. He runs to the vestibule and the heavy door that leads to the churchyard. The door is solid, and so offers no view of what lies beyond. Its solidity lends an additional disadvantage. It is soundproof. He cocks an ear to it and is rewarded only with the internal churning of blood from his inner ear.

The vestibule has a small cloakroom and Pete selects a long coat from one of the pegs. It looks as if it might belong to Father Caleb and he decides it won't be an unhelpful addition, if he's going to sneak out of the village unseen. The wood-panelled wall has a large noticeboard, advertising forthcoming events, a raffle, a prayer meeting, a cake sale. All very wholesome stuff. No mention of satanic rituals.

To one side there is a framed picture of Father Caleb alongside his stony-faced second-in-command, Margaret. Next to it is a much older picture. In the corner there is a date scratched into the sepia photograph. It says 1 April 1912. The man who stands stoically in front of the entrance to Little Baddington church looks familiar, but there is no doubting who the woman standing at his side is. It is Margaret.

Pete thinks about what Margaret said, about not fearing death. He thinks about Tom's resurrection and wonders if even his Glock offers a realistic chance of escape. A wave of hopelessness threatens to overwhelm him. He wrestles that feeling to the floor. It is harder to do than he would have liked. This is not the time for Why or even How, he thinks. Neither will help him.

There must be another way out, thinks Pete, one that'll give him the opportunity to check the ground ahead as opposed to walking straight into the arms of Noah and his shotgun. He heads to the rear of the church and sees a small door, to the left of the altar. It is unlocked and opens stiffly against the stone floor. It reveals a small office. There are bundles of swollen papers scattered across on a desk and piled high on the floor, all fruited with mildew. It smells like the crypt, rich with mould and decay.

There isn't a door to the outside, but there is a small metal-framed glazed window that Pete thinks he might be able to wriggle through. He drags a chair over to it, steps up and forces it open. A brief snowstorm of rust peppers his face. The air outside bites his skin but is welcome compared to the stench of the room. He tosses the axe through the window, hearing it thump onto grass. The shotgun follows. He hauls himself through one-handed, doing his best to protect his stump. He drops to the ground and freezes, listening intently. He hears a distant hum of conversation followed by a spike of bright laughter wholly out of keeping with his predicament.

The villagers are busy, it seems. It's time to see with what.

Chapter 18

Father Caleb runs a worried hand across his face. Its rough passage over his skin does little to restore any sense of calm to his thoughts. He stands over the beheaded corpse of Ezekiel. An ink blot of blood has formed on the floor. He is unable to interpret any pattern in its meandering shape, beyond the obvious fact that it spells trouble. The edges of it have started to coagulate and soon it will be fixed in shape and form, as will his destiny if he cannot reacquire Pete Collins. He casts a helpless glance at Noah and Joe, which bounces back like a failed signal.

Margaret joins them. She leans forward to study Zeke's corpse.

'So, where is he?' she says.

'Don't know, but he can't have gone far. Zeke's still warm,' says Noah.

'You need to find him, and quickly. You and Joseph, go now, search the village. You have weapons? Caleb says you have his gun?' says Margaret. She hasn't taken her eyes off Zeke, and her stillness is making them all nervous.

'I've got it,' says Noah. He pulls the Glock out of his pocket. 'I'll get the bastard, we'll get him, won't we, Joe, he won't get away.'

'I know you will, Noah, but bring him back in one piece, do you understand? You can put a hole in him, if you have to, but I need him alive, if he's dead, then we will have.... other problems...' Margaret allows her words to settle. She knows

Noah is bright enough to understand the subtext. His brother less so, but he'll do as he is told. Everyone knows Joe would follow Noah to the ends of the earth and off the edge, if his brother asked him to. Such loyalty is useful.

'Then go, and may our Lord protect you in your work,' says Margaret.

The two brothers hurry out of the church, leaving Margaret with Caleb.

'We better move Ezekiel's body,' says Caleb. 'It won't do for anyone else to see him.'

'Yes,' says Margaret. 'You better move his body, Caleb. It seems I have another of your messes to tidy up.' Her voice is soft and deadly.

'It's not my fault...' he splutters.

'It never is, is it, Caleb, but if not you then who? Zeke? You wear that robe of office so well, but rarely seem to feel its weight...'

Caleb opens and closes his mouth like a fish, thinks better of any further retort, and sets about picking up Zeke by the ankles and dragging him to the back of the church. A crimson trail of blood smears the floor behind him.

'Consider your task a simple one, Caleb. Clean that mess up afterwards. I will go and speak to our Lord and explain what's happened. Let us pray he doesn't require immediate recompense for our failings.'

Caleb's face goes a ghostly white. 'Of course, Margaret, of course. I serve you and the Lord, he who walks in the furrows...' he says.

Margaret nods, steals herself and opens the door to the crypt.

****

Pete hasn't got far. Only moments after he'd exited via the back window he spots Father Caleb swaggering back to the church. A cry of alarm reciprocated a hasty and less confident demeanour when he stumbles back to the village to gather up a gang of helpers. He returns with Noah and Joseph. Margaret arrives a few minutes later, a sour expression set like concrete on her face.

His stump is bleeding. The wax cap that Margaret applied has fractured, allowing blood to ooze out of the makeshift dressing. The flow is steady enough to be a problem. He needs to tourniquet his arm. He leans against the wall of the church, hidden in shadow, and uses his knife to cut a strip of material from his shirt. He ties it around his upper arm, pulling the cloth tight with his teeth, ignoring the pain. The flow of blood eases, for now, and for now is all he needs.

Noah and Joseph leave the church, walking with purpose, telegraphing 'men on a mission' vibes, Pete's Glock in Noah's hand. They exit through the gate, and he watches them stop in the road, exchanging brief words and a pat on the shoulder, before separating. Joseph walks towards the village green, which is now busy with people. Pete can see a stage around the maypole and a flash of smiling faces in the flickering torchlight. The small crowd hums with expectation.

That Glock is Pete's ticket out of Little Baddington. He needs to get it back, and efficiently. That makes Noah his number one target. He's gone the opposite direction to

Joseph, away from the green and up the hill towards the pub.

He glides across the graveyard, moving swiftly between the trees. It's good to be moving again, hunting rather than being hunted, and with prey that feels entirely familiar. He decides not to think about the creature in the crypt, he'll focus on what he knows. Killing folks. He's good at that, he reminds himself. Noah's already halfway up the hill. The light from the torches diminishes up there, and so Pete gets moving, before he vanishes into the darkness.

****

Father Caleb steels himself outside the door to the crypt, like a naughty pupil called to see a headmaster. He can hear movement within and low voices. He has put Ezekiel's corpse in the old office. The open window and chair beneath it giving a clear indication of how Pete Collins made his escape. He wants to tell Margaret what he's discovered but can't bring himself to disturb her.

Their god is fully awake now, that much is clear, and his displeasure is palpable. It infects the air around him, a pervasive fog riven with anger. The paralysis it brings finds a willing bedfellow, allowing his hand to hover ineffectually over the door handle. Caleb knows blood must be spilled to sate appetite and fulfil promises. He wonders what further bargains Margaret might be striking behind the door. Things have gone smoothly for some time, long enough to forget what's at stake if it went wrong. He hears footsteps and hastily backs away from the door, lest he is found eavesdropping.

The door opens and Margaret appears. There is a smell from within, animalistic, like a lion's den at the zoo. Her face is flushed and youthful. Her eyes wild. Caleb shrinks before her.

'We have reached an accommodation,' she breathes. 'At least for now, and it is, I think, a fair one.'

'Good news…..may I ask what it is?' says Caleb. His smile is sickly.

'Well,' says Margaret, her voice dipped in acid. 'You will go and help Noah and Joe find our sacrifice, and I will head up to our lovely pub and find an acceptable alternative.'

'Penny!?' says Caleb, with rather more force than he intended. More softly he says, 'I mean, are you sure, she is one of us now, we discussed how useful new blood is for the village. We are old, the women barren, she offers opportunity for a future… more for our Lord's trip…surely there is an alternative?'

'She offers many things, but blood, for now, is what we require, unless of course you wish to place your precious neck on the block in her stead?' says Margaret.

Caleb drops his head, staring at his shoes.

'I thought not,' says Margaret. 'Now go and find Mr Collins, and maybe there is a chance your precious Penny will survive the night…'

Caleb scurries to the door, leaving Margaret in the dim silence of the church. Her legs still tremble from the memory of her Lord's touch. Her Lord could be cruel, but he bestowed love on those that showed loyalty, devotion, obedience.

Silently, she too had hoped for better use of Penny. She didn't like her, but that wasn't a barometer for usefulness. Her womb was meant to improve the gene pool of the village, another downside of the insularity she has fostered. New blood was required if the village was to endure, notwithstanding their god's regenerative abilities. It worked, of that there was no doubt, the simple passing of years was no longer a limiting factor. But it didn't last forever. The fading strength of Lord Baddington, holed up in his manor house, a skeletal, ephemeral presence, holding on to life only with the vicious determination of one who'd never been denied anything in his privileged life, was testament to that fact, as were the barren wombs of the women in the village who'd taken the sacrament. They lived on, but the eggs in their bellies withered and died, like everything else.

Margaret takes a deep breath. She has work to do, and then, with the blessing of he who walks the furrows, the night will be won.

****

Penny floats across the empty dining room of The Yew Tree on an updraught of pure anxiety.

There is a celebration tonight, a special one according to Father Caleb, and she has instructions to attend, but Craig hasn't returned home. He'd left her earlier that morning, his trajectory prompted by harsh words and recrimination, but it has been over ten hours now, and her certainty about who was right and who was wrong is being sorely tested.

Their argument wasn't new. It is the same one they've been swatting back and forth for months, a tennis rally that refuses to end. He wants to leave. She wants to stay.

Little Baddington is a wedge between them, one that she's enthusiastically applied pressure to, deliberately forcing a moment of breakage. She regrets her actions now, as she regrets almost everything about their ill-fated decision to move from Hampstead. She is no longer sure they were happy before, but the move here accelerated the decline, triggering a continental drift that's now passed a point of no return.

Craig had told her she was to stop going to the church. He'd said it was unhealthy. He said she was getting as crazy as the rest of them. He said it was meant to be them versus the world, she wasn't meant to switch sides. Penny's not sure when she did switch sides, but ruefully admits to herself that she has. She wonders if it's even possible to go back.

The door opens, and Margaret enters. She radiates a crazed excitement, transmitting it like a virus before her. It amplifies her size, making her scrawny frame fill the empty room. Penny's always been wary of Margaret, most of the villagers are, albeit concerns are unspoken, portrayed on that telepathic frequency reserved for mutual self-preservation. Tonight, the sense of wrested control, a begrudging obligation to carry on a fiction of normality, has been discarded. Margaret looks unleashed. She has the eyes of someone who is losing control and enjoying every moment of it.

'Margaret,' says Penny. 'What brings you here? I was just about to leave. Is something the matter?'

'Is something the matter? Yes....yes....I believe there is something the matter, dear Penny...' Margaret's mouth puckers over her name, as if it tastes bad.

'Oh no! Can.... can I help you..?'

Margaret passes a hand across her face, and, like a mime, reveals an entirely new expression, one shrouded in cold calm that is infinitely more unsettling than the fevered excitement that preceded it.

'Oh yes, my dear, you most certainly can,' she says with undisguised relish. A hand closes tightly around Penny's arm and Margaret can feels bones grinding. She enjoys the moment. Penny's fear is palpable. She can taste it and it is delicious. Suffering, in whatever form it takes, is her drug of choice, although she prefers to acknowledge that feeling as one of holy exaltation, a consequence of doing the Lord's work. Sometimes she dreams of a fire, within it dancing the tallow corpses of those who've wronged her. She awakens, flushed, sweaty, and satisfied.

'You're hurting me,' says Penny.

'Am I?' says Margaret. 'I'm sorry about that.' She pulls Penny towards the door, her grip undiminished.

'Where are you taking me? Where's Father Caleb?' says Penny.

'Put on your coat, dear, all will be revealed,' says Margaret. She offers a smile constipated with falsehood. 'Come, come, no time for delay! The evening's festivities are about to begin. We don't want you to miss them!'

Penny snatches a glance at the empty restaurant and bar and can't help wondering if she is seeing it for the last time. The cold air outside snaps those thoughts from her head. Down the hill, the village green crackles with activity. The small crowd of villagers has arranged itself into loose concentric circles around the stage. They're not holding hands and swaying yet, but it looks as though that is in the post.

Penny experiences a blast of icy clarity, as if she is being dragged out of a fog. 'Where's Craig?' she asks, 'I need to see Craig.'

'Craig?' says Margaret. 'Of course.' Her smile broadens. 'He's in the church. He's been helping us. He's been very helpful in fact. You can see him soon, but first let's get you down to the green, with all your new friends. You can meet up with Craig after, when the party is finished, yes?'

The grip on Penny's arm offers no alternative. Margaret closes the door behind them. Penny is escorted dutifully across the path to the road. Music strikes up, a soft melody of intertwining chords that is oddly disorientating, making every step seem like one that transports you back in time.

'Come, Penny, no time to dawdle. Your audience awaits,' says Margaret.

****

Pete pulls the hood of his borrowed robe up over his head and walks casually up the road after Noah. His stride is steady and assured. He looks neither left nor right but makes sure it doesn't look as though he is neither looking left nor right either. The crowded village green passes him by on his left. Strange ephemeral music starts, adding to the sense of dislocation he feels, as if Little Baddington is a bubble within time, one whose walls are thin, and the past is pushing hungrily in.

Noah is now twenty paces ahead of him, heading towards The Yew Tree. His battered Land Rover, the one that had transported him to the church what seems like a million years ago, is the lone vehicle in the car park. The uplights that illuminate the pub have been switched off, and it broods in the darkness. Pete decides the car park is the place to deal with Noah, and he allows ice to flow into his veins. The karambit sits in his hand. Craig's blood has dried, soon it'll be mixed with Noah's.

He hears Noah grunt, 'Margaret,' as two figures materialise out of the dark to his right. He catches a glimpse of Penny's face, ghostly white, eyes dripping with fear. They fix on his own, flashing both recognition and warning. Pete's heart rears up like a horse in his chest. They hurry past him, Penny woven within Margaret's fevered grip.

She could've called him out, but she didn't.

His hand tightens on the knife.

He wonders if he might have to take Penny with him. But first...Noah.

Chapter 19

The rise and swell of music amongst the villagers becomes a dreamy carousel. They join hands, allowing rhythm to move them back and forth as one. Expectant faces turn to the stage. They wait for Margaret and Father Caleb to join them and tell them what to do.

Father Caleb appears, his face the colour of nightmares. He crosses the road on unsteady feet. Behind him, in the churchyard, the yew trees rustle and sway, displaced by something unseen. The two goats, tethered to the maypole, bleat a welcome as two huge cloven hoofs sink deep into green turf. The village turns with a collective sigh of welcome. Each sees what they want to see, what they need to see, as is a god's glamour, a god's deceit, where honey pours into the ear; and scales are cast across eyes.

The child of Baphomet has grown into adulthood. It towers over Father Caleb, who walks on borrowed legs ahead of it, his head high and eyes maniacal with a caustic mix of devotion and terror. Its legs are covered in coarse brown hair that rise above cloven feet. The hair thins at its waist where the legs join a human torso, thick and muscular. Its arms hang, apelike, impossibly long and powerful. Its head is that of a goat, its horns have sprouted like corn, curling around its skull, which is dense across the brow and forehead.

The circle of hands formed by the villagers parts like cotton, and Father Caleb enters. He looks towards the maypole, sees only Herschel, and feels a rising tide of displeasure build in the air behind him. He maintains a beatific smile for the benefit of his congregation, nodding here and there in recognition, barely seeing any faces amidst the panic that burns beneath his scalp.

Heavy hands settle on his shoulders. He feels tattered nails rest on his skin, encrusted with filth and dried blood that squirms with unknowable things. Their presence promises only pain and suffering. He whimpers, silently praying for Margaret to materialise with Penny. He would happily cut Penny's throat himself if it meant these bestial hands would be removed from him.

Father Caleb draws Herschel towards him. 'The fucking goats,' he hisses. 'Get the fucking goats.'

'The, the goats...?' stutters Herschel.

'Yes, the fucking goats, now...now!' he almost screams. The goats won't be nearly enough. The tightening grip on his shoulders provides confirmation. He feels hot bovine breath at his ear. The god grinds bastardized words out of its disfigured mouth, the sound like gravel hitting the bottom of a tin bucket. *'Where......is.......it....'*

Margaret pushes her way through the crowd, Penny is at her side. Father Caleb finds he can breathe again.

****

Noah pauses. He's about ten feet away from his Land Rover but senses something isn't right. He can feel a presence the way a fox tastes a rabbit within a night breeze. Noah spins around, the Glock rising in his hand. Seconds elongate into minutes.

The knife flies from Pete's hand. The gun's blank eye flashes in the night and Pete feels heat burn across his cheek. The karambit hits its target with a meaty thud. Noah stumbles backwards as if shoved by a mighty hand. The Glock falls to the ground with a metallic clatter. Pete rushes forward; he stoops, drops his shoulder, and connects with Noah's midriff, knocking him to the floor with a whooping gasp of air. Pete rolls on the gravel, trying to protect his right arm. His feet scramble for purpose. Noah groans thickly. He's trying to grab the knife that is embedded in his shoulder, but the handle is slick with his blood. The Glock sits on the ground between them, and their eyes meet. There is a moment of perfect understanding. Noah bares his teeth and growls like a dog.

Pete gets there first. The Glock is homecoming in his hand. He doesn't hesitate. The retort of the pistol is blunt. The back of Noah's skull is blown across the gravel. He slumps to the ground, dead.

Pete brings his hand to his face and winces. *Another injury to add to the list*, he thinks. The bullet has ploughed a deep furrow in his cheek. It fills with blood and runs down his neck, soaking the collar of his shirt.

The Glock has four bullets left in the clip. The shotgun has four rounds, giving him a grand total of eight. He thinks about Penny, who just wanted to belong somewhere, and somehow managed to put her chips on the worst possible number in life's casino. *Fuck it*, he thinks, *fuck it*. He looks back down the hill and knows where he must go. Besides, he thinks, he has a score to settle with Margaret and Caleb.

****

The first of Joseph's goats gargles, as blood splatters the floor from the mouth opened at its throat. With a grunt of effort, Herschel heaves the carcass off the ground, holding it by its hind legs in a ham-sized fist. The tip of his knife finds the goat's belly, peeling the skin and tissue apart. An unborn kid drops to the stage with a splat, followed by a ribbon of guts that steam gently in the cold air. The embryonic goat mewls softly. The goat's companion bleats from its place, tied beneath the maypole.

Father Caleb reaches down and digs around in the bloody mess at his feet. He lifts the slick foetus. Herschel slices the umbilical cord, untethering it from its dead mother. He raises it above his head, as blood runs down his arm.

Margaret pushes Penny onto the stage. She stumbles and falls to her knees. 'Please,' breathes Penny. 'Please don't do this, don't...?' Margaret kneels in front of her, placing a hand under Penny's chin, gently encouraging her gaze to meet her own. Her thumb draws a line down her forehead in blood. 'Don't be afraid, child. This is your chance to truly belong. Isn't that what you always wanted?'

The crowd sighs, transfixed as tears roll down Penny's face, burning bright in the torchlight. 'I don't...I don't understand, where's Craig? What's happening?'

'Don't cry, Penny dear. You will be with him soon...begin!' cries Margaret.

Herschel drags Penny to her feet, takes her by the arm and enthusiastically starts to bind her to the maypole. Maria joins him in his work. She croons in Penny's ear, soft lullabies whose words make Penny want to scream. She pushes a lock of hair from Penny's brow like an attentive mother and kisses her forehead farewell.

Margaret stands at the heel of her god. She is breathless in its presence, feeling heat in parts of her body that are normally cold and barren. She licks her lips, reaching out a hand touching the thick wiry hair that adorns its muscular legs. She shivers with delight. She can't wait to see what the wire will do to Penny's pale, fragile skin. She can't wait to see what the god will do to her broken body.

'Kill the bitch!' screams Doc Brown from the crowd. His cry is taken up by others.

Humanity retreats from Little Baddington, leaving hell in its wake.

All praise he who walks in the furrows, thinks Margaret as a lightning strike orgasm wracks her body.

Chapter 20

Pete runs down the hill on soft feet, the Glock easy in his hand. His knife is in a pocket, and the shotgun is slung across his back. He thinks he must look quite a sight, and no longer cares who sees him. The time for discretion has passed. The blood that drains from his body foreshadows weakness. He fears his life can now be measured by the number of bullets in his Glock.

The torches that surround the green have dimmed, but the air thrums with excited shouting. The maypole is the centre of the commotion. He can pick out the shapes of people struggling, and amongst them there is something else. Unformed, but huge. It flickers in and out of his vision, as if his eyes are protecting him from the truth.

New movement springs up, rhythmic and precise, a circular dance. Pete sees people weaving between each other, in and out. The disconnected music has stopped but this rhythm seems well established. The air fizzes with expectation as the circles they create become tighter, closing in on the maypole.

****

Penny has lost capacity to feel pain. She sees a spiral of cavorting faces, a blur of white teeth, red smiles, and dead eyes. With every rotation, razor wire cuts deeper into her skin. As it reaches its epicentre, criss-crossing her legs, torso and arms, it forces her clothing into her flesh, tighter and tighter until both cloth and skin capitulate. The ground at her feet is painted red. A few more turns around the maypole will bring the wire to her neck and face.

Through a haze of agony, she sees Margaret's triumphant gaze. The Custodian of Little Baddington church, the power behind the throne, is hungry for suffering.

The wire climbs to her throat and Penny closes her eyes.

****

Pete can see what's happening and has seen enough.

Two men stand beside guttering torches, twenty to thirty feet apart along the perimeter of the green. Shotguns are casually slung over arms and shoulders, as they enjoy the show. The crowd offers up a collective gasp and the distraction is timely. The man nearest Pete cranes his neck to get look at what is happening, and Pete's on him in a heartbeat. The karambit slices his throat and Pete gently guides his spluttering body to the floor.

To his immediate left, the other man looks across, his face a study in confusion. Pete can see his brain whirring into life. His shotgun swings off his shoulder. Pete drops, brings up the Glock and shoots. The man's head explodes, and he collapses to the floor.

Pete knows momentum is a precarious commodity. It will start to swing away from him if he doesn't capitalise on what little he has gained. He doesn't have a plan as such, just the notion that they are all going to pay for what they've done. It's oddly liberating to operate with such freedom. He isn't beholden to contract, to instruction. Only to himself and what he thinks is right.

His gunshot hasn't gone unnoticed by the crowd. Some turn to see what is happening. Someone screams a warning. Pete dives amongst them, swimming through the excited throng.

He spots Father Caleb cast a wary glance towards the commotion, but Pete dips low, pushing forward in his long dark coat.

The crowd's attention returns to the stage. Penny is suspended from the maypole, held by wires that criss-cross deep inside her body. Her torso is awash with blood. If she's not dead already, then she soon will be. Pete's stomach clenches like a fist. He casts a snatched glance over his shoulder. Time is short. Somewhere along the way he has lost the shotgun. He has three bullets left in his Glock.

Father Caleb approaches Penny, gently lifts her head so her pale face can be seen by the crowd. A bubble of blood forms at her lips, and he wonders if it holds her last breath.

'My friends,' he calls. His voice is strong and carries across the heads of the crowd, muting its febrile hum by inches. 'This night has brought us together, for the love of our Lord, he who walks in the furrows, who brings us his sanctity, and binds us within his loving embrace...' He pauses, allowing the words to settle. 'The year has been long,' he says, shaking his head sadly. 'And each to come will grow longer still, unless we continue to fight for our little piece of home, safe in the furrows..'

The crowd murmurs its response '.... In the furrows...'

'We do what is right for us, safe in the knowledge that we will be protected by our Lord...'

'.... In the furrows....'

'So now we gather, on All Hallows' Eve, as we do each year, to pay homage to our Lord, to provide him with testament, with our tribute, so he will keep watch over us for another year, safe in the furrows...'

'...In the furrows...' they cry, more lustily this time.

Pete stands, momentarily transfixed. The crowd is heating up, feeding off the rhythm of Caleb's words. He feels resistance around him, an unwillingness to make room. A crescendo is approaching, the eager sense of something not to be missed.

'Sacrifice!!' screams Father Caleb, spittle flying from his lips.

'Sacrifice!!' chimes the crowd hungrily.

A shadow passes over the crowd, hushing it into subservience. The great goat god lurches out of the night and takes its place at the maypole. The crowd gasps in delight as its ragged figure, dripping hunger, sniffs Penny's slumped body. Pete feels like a mountaineer who hears the distant rumble of avalanche. There is a change in the air around him, a dropping of the mercury that ignites heat in his stomach even as it chills the skin on his arms, which has raised into gooseflesh.

'For it is the will of our Lord to take what is due, to replenish his spirit so he can hold us dear and close for the cold months that follow. We give homage to our Lord, let us pray and bless his feasting...'

The crowd drops to their knees and Pete is left exposed like a piling at low tide.

****

Margaret's eyes widen as she sets eyes on Pete. She drives her elbow into Caleb's side, who turns and follows her gaze. He looks like a man who's discovered a winning lottery ticket hasn't gone in the bin after all.

'Grab him!' she screams. 'Grab him, there – him, get him!'

A scattering of the prostrated crowd raise their bowed heads. Pete snatches the seconds their confusion offers. He takes aim at Caleb, but a stray elbow nudges him and his shot flies high and wide. The retort triggers panic and some people start to run. An old man with a crop of fuzzy grey hair lurches at him and he plants a bullet between his eyes, blowing a liberal amount of blood and brains over the scattering crowd. Someone screams, 'Doc!'

Two bullets left.

Herschel charges towards him, swinging his meat cleaver before him. Space clears around him, as if he's a shark swimming through a shoal of sardines. Pete can't get a clear shot, and his hesitation allows Herschel to get in close, where he wants to be. The cleaver swipes through the air, missing him by inches. Pete kicks Herschel's thigh, eliciting a grunt of pain, but he shows no sign of stopping. He's like the tide, he just keeps on coming.

Pete knows he's swiftly losing whatever small advantage he has. Herschel is big and horribly strong, but his blind rage makes him vulnerable. It's like fighting a wrecking ball, if he can avoid the swing, he might find an opening. Herschel's cleaver carves the night air again, but the momentum of his attack takes his legs from under him, and he topples to his knees. Pete hooks his severed forearm around his neck, brings the Glock up under Herschel's chin and lets it go. The top of his skull explodes like a champagne cork. Pete hears Maria's scream, high and reedy and totters back on his heels, his head suddenly levitating. Maria drops to the floor, in a dead faint. The goat god eyes her curiously before returning its attention to its meal.

There is more trouble coming. A bearded man approaches from his right, teeth bared. Pete feels blood pooling at his waist, Herschel's blade has caught him after all. Pete has one bullet left in his Glock and doesn't think this man is worthy of it. He beckons him forward, hanging his head low, sure his bloodstained appearance will give this idiot the overconfidence he needs to acquaint him with the karambit. It works. He launches himself at him and as a simple roll of his shoulder throws the man off balance, he spins past Pete and falls to the floor. Pete is on him, grabbing his long greasy hair and yanking up his head. His knife opens a mouth in his throat.

A shotgun blast punches the air. An old woman collapses to the floor next to Pete, her face a bloody red mass. Screams fill the air, and the village green descends into chaos.

Chapter 21

'What do we do?' shouts Father Caleb. 'This....this is madness.' He gestures helplessly at the screaming crowd. 'The village, all we've done. It will be lost...'

'Stiffen your back, Caleb,' snaps Margaret. 'You whimper like a dog. It is unbecoming of a man of God.'

'Look at what he's done...Herschel is dead. So many dead. He's a killer.'

'And so are we, unless you've forgotten,' she snaps in reply. 'Look, Joseph returns. We outnumber him. He is dying as we speak.'

Pete does indeed look like a dead man walking. He staggers across the green on legs that waver like saplings in a stiff breeze.

'And do not forget, our Lord is here for us, and that man there is his prize. Do you think it'll be given up so easily?'

Margaret welcomes the blank obedience that once again floods Caleb's broad face. He nods. Behind them, the child of Baphomet busily crunches its way through what's left of Penny's body. It tugs at a tattered arm, as if pulling hay from a bale, seemingly oblivious to the chaos that unfolds.

****

Joseph's face is blank, he sees only his dead brother, who he found shoved beneath his Land Rover, like he'd been fly-tipped.

A screaming woman, who he dimly recognises a teacher from the school, clutches at him, and he brings the butt of his shotgun onto her chin. She falls to the floor with a whining thump. Ahead of him, he sees the man who killed his brother. He holds a gun in a hand that is bloody with guilt. Joseph bares his teeth, raises his shotgun and fires.

Pete feels heat in his side before the blast of the shotgun roars in his ears. He stumbles, the grass suddenly slick with his blood. His breath whistles between gritted teeth. He feels his legs give way, buckling at the knee like wet cardboard. He hits the floor, his Glock wedged beneath him. Joseph strides towards him with an executioner's tread. He is reloading his shotgun and the noise of the shotgun hinge clicking shut is far louder than it should be. The dead eyes of its barrel stare down at him, mirroring those of its owner.

'You killed my brother, you fuck...I'm going to kill you...'

'Joseph!!!' shouts Margaret. 'Stop! His life is not yours to take! Justice will be served, Joseph. But not like this. Our Lord, this one is promised to him. And then, with his grace, we can revive your brother, he can come back to us, but first you must step down, and allow our Lord to take him, as was planned.'

Joseph snarls. The shotgun wavers in his hand but its gaze remains steadfast on Pete's prone body.

'Joseph, please, for the good of the village, step back,' says Caleb. 'Our Lord awaits, see...he watches over us...he watches you...'

Joseph's head lifts, as if on strings. There is a hulking shape behind Margaret. It fills him with a soft dread that creeps up from his stomach and infects his thoughts. He doesn't want to give this man to their god, he only wants to kill him, avenge his brother, and beyond that, well, he doesn't care.

'I serve no god,' he says softly. Joseph steadies his shotgun, his finger eases onto the trigger.

Margaret springs at him like a malevolent jack-in-the-box. She has retrieved Herschel's cleaver and brings it down onto Joseph's neck with all her wiry strength. The blade lodges in his shoulder bone, and she rocks it back and forth, like a woodcutter releasing an axe, before bringing it down again. Blood fountains from his neck. Joseph howls and drops his shotgun before crumpling to the floor.

Father Caleb goggles at a village green that resembles a war zone.

'Don't just stand there, you fool – get his gun!' screams Margaret.

Pete watches Father Caleb stumble past him and pick up Joe's shotgun. He breathes in the scent of grass. It feels as if he is floating, and he supposes this is what dying is, the slow release of all things, hopes, fears, ambitions, leeching out of you in tandem with the softening pump of arteries. His good arm is trapped beneath him. His fingers hold the Glock, but he can't find the strength or the will to push himself away from the embrace of the soil.

The remaining villagers have scattered, leaving the green empty. The night air grows still, save for Father Caleb's ragged breathing. 'Margaret,' he says weakly, gesturing at Joseph's body. Steam rises from the red canyon she's carved into his neck. He wonders what they have done.

'Spare me your whining regret. Mr Collins is of no use to us dead. His soul is promised. If we deliver, then all might rise again. The village will be restored, but not if we don't. It is the way of things, Caleb. Now get a grip on yourself, or I will find myself a new priest…'

Father Caleb bristles. 'We both serve the village, Margaret, the village is greater than us.'

'You serve the village, Caleb, I serve our Lord…' snaps Margaret. 'All you have done is continue good work. No more than that. The work of my father, of me, it both precedes you and exceeds you. Pride is a sin, Father…lest you forget.'

A deep gurgling growl slices their squabble in two. It's a sound you'd expect to hear from a closet in the dead of night. A great horned head looms over them. Behind it, Penny's body has been picked clean. Little remains, save a shattered ribcage and a ragged flap of skin that clings stubbornly to the tangle of wire that had held her. Their local god's lunatic mouth drips hungry saliva that fizzes on the cold soil. It contemplates Maria's prone body, sniffing it approvingly as its artic gaze flicks between Margaret and Caleb, radiating a dreadful impatience that freezes words on lips. It looks over the tangle of broken bodies that litter the village green, its nostrils flaring.

'Your congregation is… diminished,' it croaks.

'Our offering, my Lord,' says Margaret. She is babbling and hates how weak it makes her sound. 'Here it is. As promised. I have done your bidding, oh Lord, I serve you…. Caleb, help me bring it to him…. help me…..'

Father Caleb shuffles towards Margaret. 'Is he alive?' he says meekly.

'You better hope so,' she hisses. 'Grab an arm, turn him over...'

Pete holds what little breath he has left. Rough hands grab him and roll him onto his back. His Glock barks its last retort. Caleb's head disappears, painting Margaret's face red. Her mouth drops open, a perfect circle of stunned surprise.

Chapter 22

Pete offers a weak chuckle to the stars.

He is dying and doesn't care.

Margaret's face is a bloodstained mask of lunacy. She is trying to scream, but either the sound won't come or Pete's lost the capacity to hear it. She raises the meat cleaver high above her head and its blade grins at him. From somewhere, he finds the strength to flail his left arm in front of him and the cleaver thumps into it with sickening force. He watches with a strange almost detached interest as his lower arm falls onto his chest. Shattered bone juts out of his flesh, like an exclamation mark. Blood fountains enthusiastically from the ragged wound, covering his face.

Margaret pants like a mad dog. She swipes the back of her hand across her face and licks blood from her lips. Pete sees her as if through a smeared window, one thick with handprints, like the one in his bedroom when he was a boy, where he used to watch and wait for his mum to return home from work. Hoping she'd be back before Dad got back from the pub or woke up and decided to use his fists.

He thinks about how his life has led him to this point. The lives he's taken without thought, where he's only played executioner, one oblivious to judge and jury. He regrets he won't get the chance to pay back Dave and all his cronies for this fucking mess. The rest, all of it, falls aside, flashing through his consciousness as if blurred scenery on a fast train.

Margaret kicks him. 'Wake up, you fucker!' she screams. 'Wake up and face your destiny, you louse, you dog, you cur, you can't escape by dying. He will feed and you will suffer....'

She steps aside and the goat god stands over him. He can feel its interest under his scalp, light fingers probing his fading neurons, tasting his dying thoughts.

'I can build again, my Lord,' pants Margaret. 'You will never go hungry here. I promise you that. Eat...eat well, fill your stomach and leave the rest to me...'

A huge hand settles on Margaret's shoulder. She shivers with delight as it caresses her neck and moves restlessly over her hair.

'I am yours,' she breathes. 'Oh my Lord, I am yours to do with as you please...' It cradles her head in its palm. Margaret smiles dreamily, as if a comforted infant, returned to a loving mother.

The hand snaps into a fist. The sound of Margaret's skull splitting is wet and meaty. Her body seems to deflate, hanging like a forgotten party balloon from the God's clenched fist. It opens and her body drops to the grass, with all the grace of a turd slipping from a dog's arse.

The child of Baphomet squats in front of Pete, its great head tilted to one side, like an amicable coach about to impart wisdom to his team. Its odd, rectangular eyes regard him curiously. He wonders if it can hear the furtive beat of his fading heart in his chest, its presence soft, like an intruder's footstep on a stair at night.

'You bring chaos,' it growls, raising its great head and casting a satisfied gaze over the corpses that litter the village green. *'And blood......What is your name?'*

Pete's eyes close. 'Cain,' he whispers.

'He who would bring death to his brother... of course... I think you and I will do great things together.'

The child of Baphomet leans over his blood-spattered face and starts to retch.

Chapter 23

In a pub in Bromley By Bow, a man who calls himself Dave sits at a table. He has his back to the wall, and a clear view of the door. He's always been a naturally cautious man, but these days, more than ever, he appreciates a clear view of his exits.

The chair opposite him is currently occupied by a small man with ferrety features. He's a man whose shifty nature is replicated by a restless movement within his own skin. He is a sea of tics and twitches.

Dave sighs; he finds this low-level stuff dull. This man isn't a professional, he's a street rat, perfect for the type of job he currently must fill, but it's tiresome stuff. He pushes a piece of paper across the table towards him. 'The name's there. And the address. The price is the usual, non-negotiable,' says Dave. He's prepared for a brief pantomime, a tug of war to test boundaries. It'll end the way he wants. This guy has zero leverage.

'Prices have gone up. There's a cost-of-living crisis, you know,' says the ferret man, with a sly smile.

'Not around here they haven't,' says Dave evenly. 'I have other people. Take it or leave it.'

A tic beneath the ferret man's eye accelerates. He blinks rapidly. Dave hopes this guy doesn't have a thing for poker. If he does, the money on offer won't be in his pocket for long.

'I'm getting tired. It's make your mind up time,' says Dave.

The ferret man snarls and snatches up the piece of paper, giving it a cursory look. It disappears into one of the numerous pockets of his jacket. 'Payment on delivery?' he says.

'Of course.'

He pushes back his chair, runs a hand through greasy hair and saunters across the pub to the door. He doesn't look back. Dave sits back in his chair and blows air through pursed lips. He's tired. Living on your nerves can do that to you, he thinks, and living on his nerves he has been, ever since the news story about the village that disappeared, the story about Little Baddington.

The story held the headlines for a few weeks, no mean feat in these days of twenty-four-seven rolling news. Dave supposes it's not every day a whole village goes missing. They'd called it a modern-day Marie Celeste. Dave never visited the shitty little place, he never needed to, so there was a surreal, almost voyeuristic quality to watching news footage of empty houses, a deserted shop, a cavernous church that'd been burnt out, and wondering how it all fitted in with the nefarious pipeline that greedily sucked up people that needed disappearing.

Eighteen months have passed and there's been no sign of 'Pete Collins', but Dave hasn't been able to get comfortable he's dead and gone. People like him were hard to kill. He'd had some reservations at the outset, whether Little Baddington could handle him, but had contented himself with the fact they had a track record of clearing up messes, some of them bad men, tough men. They had someone or something down there that chewed them up, so he threw Pete to them and moved on.

He regrets it now. Not that he did it, Pete had screwed up, and that was the way it worked, just that he hadn't the foresight to make sure this loose end was properly tied off. It didn't suit his character, or his professional preference, and he puts it down as a mistake. Making a mistake is not something that sits easily with him.

The pub's empty, other than its overweight proprietor Wilf, who wheezes past carrying a crate of empty beer bottles that clink in time with the gentle sway of his belly. Dave gives him a small nod.

He has no further business today and doesn't fancy availing himself of another flat lager or lifeless bitter of the type Wilf has to offer.

He's thinking about leaving when an old man in a dirty trench coat enters. He wears a baseball cap that is pulled low over his face. Grey hair spills onto his shoulders, the colour of city snowfall after a day of traffic. He has a marked hunchback, big enough that it looks as if he's got a rucksack stuffed underneath his coat. His walk is stooped and deliberate. Dave thinks he's every inch the type of customer he'd expect to wander into this shithole on a Tuesday lunchtime.

He hobbles to the bar and orders a drink. Dave gives him no further thought, and contents himself with checking email on his phone. He is surprised therefore when the old man sits himself down in the seat opposite him. He looks up, eyebrow raised.

'Can I help you, old timer?' he says.

The old man says nothing. He's removed his coat and Dave notices he only has one hand. He takes a sip of his pint. Wilf is no longer behind the bar. He could've sworn he was right there, literally a moment ago, but he's vanished.

'I said, can I help you?' Impatience tightens his voice. Dave's seen enough flotsam and jetsam blow under this door, to have little time for indulging the worst of their habits. This part of London has more than its fair share of lunatics and ne'er-do-wells. The old man continues to ignore him. He starts to roll up a cigarette, one-handed, with a hypnotic dexterity that Dave finds curiously unnerving.

'Nice place you've got here,' says the old man. His voice is younger than his appearance and somehow familiar. Dave's radar is starting to ping. He has a gun inside his jacket, small calibre, discreet, but more than enough to blow this idiot's head off at close range.

'It's not my place,' he says, his voice neutral. He wonders if the old man can hear his heart, which is beating very fast.

'That right, is it?' says the old man with a smile. He looks at Dave for the first time. He has bright green eyes.

Dave's hand wanders beneath the tabletop, searching for his jacket, which he slung over the back of his chair, a decision he is now starting to regret.

'Do I know you?' says Dave. His hand locates his gun, which he clutches like a drowning man clinging to a lifebuoy. He wonders if the old man can tell what he's doing. His bright green eyes give away nothing, except maybe a quiet amusement.

'Not sure, you look familiar, s'why I sat myself down here. There's something about your face, can't quite put my finger on it.'

The cigarette has found its way into the old man's mouth. He lights it and takes a deep drag, blowing out a plume of smoke with relish.

'Bad habit, that,' says Dave. 'Those things'll kill you.' The gun now rests on Dave's knee. Its barrel pointed at the man's stomach.

'Ha! Will they now! I don't think so, not me.'

'No?' says Dave.

'Nope,' says the old man. He seems content with his answer, and continues to take deep pulls on his cigarette, which shrinks swiftly down to a dirty stub. Dave's finite patience is once again found wanting. He brings his hand up from his knee, and slowly settles it on the table. The barrel of Dave's gun glares into the old man's face. He seems undisturbed by its presence and leans forward, placing his right arm on the table. It's been severed, just above the wrist. The skin around the stump is a puckered and jarringly youthful pink.

'Lost this a while back, got myself into some trouble down country,' he says.' I miss it, sometimes at night I swear I can still feel it, the hand you know. Like it tingles. Phantom nerves, they call it.'

'I repeat, do I know you?' says Dave. His voice isn't quite steady.

'You did,' says the old man. 'But I've changed. You probably don't recognise me? Doesn't matter. I'm here to collect what's due to me, that's all. Been a long road to get here, few things to get used to, but I'm glad I've found you.'

'You do see this gun, right?' says Dave. 'It's not for show. This place, no-one's going to mind if I spread your brains across the floor. It's been done before. So tell me, old man, who the fuck are you?'

'I think you know.'

Dave fires the gun. Something rears over the old man's shoulder, amorphous and black, like smoke, and swallows the bullet. The man's stump magically regenerates, and flesh flows down from its puckered end, forming a hand. In that hand is a knife. Before Dave can even register, his gun hand is pinned to the table, the knife driven through his palm and deep into the wood beneath. He screams, more in shock than pain. His gun clatters to the floor and spins to a slow stop.

'Like magic, hey?' says the old man, with a smile. The mask he's been wearing falls away, disintegrating into atoms. 'Got myself some new skills down in Little Baddington. Useful ones too, especially in our line of work.'

'Pete, what the fuck...'

'What the fuck indeed...' He chuckles. 'I've asked myself the same question several times over the past year or so.' He flexes his hand, the one that magically grew back, like he's seeing it for the first time. 'Do you know what I found in that hellhole you sent me to?' He pauses. Dave says nothing. His eyes dart left and right, like a cornered rat. 'Well, it weren't Jesus, that's for sure. They had a whole different kind of religion cooking up in that church in Little

Baddington. Or at least they did. Before I burned it to the ground.'

'Look, I didn't know what was going on down there,' says Dave. He's speaking fast. A pool of blood has formed around his hand, and a thin river has navigated its way across the surface to the table edge, where it drips steadily onto the floor. 'You fucked up. I warned you, there's consequences. This isn't a game. You knew that. I was just doing my job. Like a professional. For Christ's sake, Pete, be professional, none of this is personal. It's business.'

'My name's not Pete,' says Pete thoughtfully. 'No need for the aliases now, I guess. It's Cain...and I know it's not personal. I get it. Unfortunately, my new boss doesn't. His contracts are all kind of personal. That's the way he likes it.'

The amorphous shape that ate a bullet earlier resurfaces on Cain's shoulder. It takes on a recognisable form. Dave's eyes widen, and his mouth drops open as if on a hinge.

'He's a local god, and we're always interested in finding new sinners to join his congregation.'

Dave doesn't have time to scream.

The End

Also by this Author:

The Nasties

The Nasties. End of Watch

The Long View

In Winter's Garden

Printed in Great Britain
by Amazon